THE MIRACLE
OF SANTA MARIA

A Fergal O'Brien Western

THE MIRACLE
OF SANTA MARIA

•

I. J. Parnham

AVALON BOOKS
NEW YORK

Published by Avalon Books,
an imprint of Thomas Bouregy & Co., Inc.
160 Madison Avenue, New York, NY 10016

Library of Congress Cataloging-in-Publication Data

Parnham, I. J.
   The miracle of Santa Maria / I. J. Parnham.
      p. cm.
   ISBN 978-0-8034-7656-1 (acid-free paper)
1. Missions—Fiction.   I. Title.
   PS3616.A763M56 2011
   813'.6—dc22
                                        2010037809

PRINTED IN THE UNITED STATES OF AMERICA
ON ACID-FREE PAPER
BY RR DONNELLEY, BLOOMSBURG, PENNSYLVANIA

Author's Note

On August 7, 1869, Professor C. A. Young traveled from Princeton to Iowa to study a total solar eclipse. He observed a green line crossing the corona's spectrum. Later the line was identified as highly ionized iron, but he theorized that he had discovered a new gas, which he named *coronium*.

Therefore the professor was keen to further his studies by observing the eclipse of July 29, 1878, which cut across North America from Texas to Montana and which was commonly referred to as the Pike's Peak eclipse.

The following fictional tale does not recount his story.

Chapter One

No injury is so bad, no ailment is so painful, no condition is so embarrassing that this amber liquid cannot cure." Fergal O'Brien held a bottle of his tonic aloft. The amber liquid inside caught the rays of the sun and dappled light across the faces of the gathered crowd. "It's a universal remedy to cure all ills. And it costs only a dollar!"

Standing on the small stage he'd erected outside Shinbone's bank, Fergal cast his measured gaze along the front row of potential customers. Despite his honest smile, he received an equally measured series of skeptical glares, and he wasn't surprised when Jim Reed, who had already heckled him several times, stepped forward to sneer at him.

"That tonic isn't worth a dollar," Jim said with his hands set on his hips in a truculent manner. "I reckon the only thing it's likely to do is make you ill."

"If you buy a bottle," Fergal said, ignoring the accuracy

of Jim's assessment, "I assure you the effect will astound you so much that it'll make you believe in miracles."

Jim snorted. "I already believe in miracles. I heard that Maria in Sundown performed a miracle only last week when she cured old Rory Benson of his boils. And she didn't charge nothing!"

"So you only heard about this, but did you actually see this woman cure his boils?"

"I didn't, but—"

"Did anyone see her perform this miracle?" Fergal paced back and forth while glaring at each person in the crowd in turn, defying anyone to claim they had. "I thought not, but what I offer here will perform a miracle before your very eyes this very afternoon."

Jim looked around the crowd, meeting many eyes while licking his lips with barely suppressed glee, as if he was about to say something amusing.

"So," he said when he had everyone's attention, "are you claiming your tonic is as miraculous as the rest of your exhibits?"

As a round of appreciative laughter sounded, Fergal cast a worried glance at his fellow showman Woody, who had just finishing packing away the exhibits they'd displayed earlier. Woody returned a cold-eyed glare in a moment of shared exasperation at the failure of the townsfolk to respond favorably to the show they had laid on.

Their display of authentic historical memorabilia

had been received with derision after Jim had kindly pointed out that General Lee's battle uniform was definitely not dark blue. And they had had to abandon that part of the show completely when Woody had accidentally smudged the wet paint on the plank taken from the *Mayflower*.

So before they ended the show with Woody's presentation of his prize exhibit, the Treasure of Saint Woody, Fergal had moved on to trying to sell bottles of his tonic to cure all ills, so far without success.

He needed to impress these people quickly before they lost interest and wandered off. So he fixed his gaze on a quiet tall man in the back row of the gathered people. He stared at him for several seconds and then raised his arms.

"Does anyone here have a terrible affliction I can cure to convince you that miracles do happen?"

For long moments nobody moved. Then the man at the back raised a hand.

"I've got a terrible affliction," he said, his declaration making everyone turn to look at him. "Would your miraculous tonic cure me of it?"

"It sure would." Fergal beckoned vigorously for the man to approach. "Step up, good man, and tell everyone who you are."

"I'm Randolph McDougal," the man said as he threaded his way through the people.

"And what is your affliction?"

Randolph neatly sidestepped the last two people in the front row to stand before the stage.

"I'm blind," he said.

As the crowd provided a sympathetic sigh, Fergal stopped his enthusiastic beckoning and held out a hand, ready to grab Randolph's arm and help him up onto the stage. But with two sprightly paces and a leap with un-erring accuracy Randolph jumped up onto the stage to join him.

"And how long have you been unable to see any-thing?" Fergal asked.

Randolph looked him in the eye. "All my life."

This comment gathered another sigh from everyone in the crowd except for Jim, who provided a derisory snort.

"That's terrible," Fergal said, as Randolph picked out Jim from the crowd and cast him a harsh glare.

"It sure is." Randolph turned back to Fergal to be confronted by an even harsher glare.

"And what's it like being blind," Fergal said, speaking slowly, "and not being able to see anything at all, not the crowd, me, or even this tonic?"

Randolph winced. "It's terrible. It's been as dark as the night ever since I remember. Not that I know what the dark looks like, seeing as how I'm blind."

"Well, if you were to drink my tonic, which since you're my first customer will be free, you'll get to enjoy the light for the first time."

Fergal held out the bottle. Randolph moved for it, but then checked himself, jerked his hand to the side, and punched Fergal in the stomach.

"Sorry," he said. "Being blind is difficult."

Fergal murmured sympathetically and then slapped the bottle into Randolph's hand while rubbing his stomach with the other hand.

"Just make sure you drink the whole bottle."

Randolph faced the gathering, and then uncorked and upended the tonic. The amber liquid bubbled as it slipped into his mouth.

When he'd emptied the bottle, he wiped his mouth with the back of his hand. Then he blinked rapidly. He looked at his hand. He turned it over and then back again before screeching. He staggered backward until he walked into the wagon at the back of the stage. He reeled away while holding out a hand for Fergal to steady him. Then he looked to the sky.

"I can see!" he declared.

"It's a miracle," Fergal said.

"It sure is." Randolph shook Fergal's hand. "I would have gladly paid a dollar for this cure, but you are truly a great man to have done this worthy deed for nothing. I don't know how I can ever repay you."

"You don't need to. The sight of your happy face is enough for me." Fergal turned to the crowd and lowered his voice. "Although the second miracle will cost a dollar."

Cheers arose as everyone enjoyed the sight of Randolph wandering around pointing out all the things he could now see. But Jim shook his head.

"That's not as convincing a miracle as Maria performs," he said. "How do we know that man—?"

"Tell me, Randolph," Fergal shouted, drowning Jim out before he could cast doubt on his miraculous cure, "now that you can see, what would you like to do next?"

"I'm excited by my first sight of the exhibits in your show. They sure do look authentic to me, but this one fascinates me the most." Randolph pointed at a casket on the back of the wagon. "What is it?"

Woody took that as his cue to step forward.

"This casket contains the Treasure of Saint Woody," he said, "and you could win that treasure this very afternoon for a small investment of—"

"There can't be no real saint's treasure in there," Jim shouted.

"And why not?" Fergal snapped, swirling round to face him.

"For a start, there is no saint called Woody."

"How do you know that?"

"I know plenty about saints. In fact, many people say that one day Maria will become a saint." Jim's voice became wistful. "After all the miracles she's performed in Sundown, many people already call her Santa Maria."

"Santa Maria!" Fergal muttered, his exasperation finally bubbling over. He leaned forward to glare at Jim.

"I've heard enough of her. So tell me, where is Sundown, the home of this most blessed of ladies?"

Hank Kelly and his associates, Vernon Black and Seymour Cook, were thirty miles out of Sundown when they stopped to water their horses. Earlier they'd been run out of Shinbone after one too many punch-ups in Milton's Saloon and so they were in particularly surly moods.

When Hank saw smoke spiraling up into the afternoon sky farther downriver, he sent Vernon to investigate. With much grumbling, Vernon wandered off, but when he returned he was sporting a smile.

"It's just one man," he said. "And he doesn't look like trouble."

"Then let's give him some," Hank said.

Vernon chuckled with malicious glee. Then, in a line, the three men trotted off in the direction of the smoke.

Closer to the campsite, they saw that the solitary man was thin and graying at the temples. While his horse mooched beside the river, he worried over a tin of water he'd placed on the fire. With short darts of his head, he started at every birdcall or rustle that came from the scrub around him.

Best of all, he wasn't packing a gun.

When the advancing horses' hooves clattered over a patch of pebbles, the man flinched and then jumped to his feet to face them. Hank raised his hat and smiled.

"We'd be obliged if we could join you," he said.

"You're welcome," the man said, his weak voice shaking. He glanced over his shoulder at the vast plain behind him and shivered despite the afternoon heat. "I'm Oliver Rhinehart."

"And we're three helpful passersby."

"Then you might be able to help me. I hadn't planned to stop here for long. I hope to get to Sundown today."

"Sundown is three hours of steady riding," Hank said. "But on foot it's ten hours."

Vernon chuckled. "And if someone broke your legs it'd take a whole lot longer."

Oliver gulped. "Thank you for your advice. I have coffee, but no food to share. Like I said, I don't plan on sleeping under the stars tonight."

"But I still reckon you've got plenty to share." Hank rolled from the saddle and stalked around the fire to stand beside Oliver's horse. He patted the bulky saddlebags. "Let's see what you've got."

Oliver jumped to his feet and scurried toward Hank, but Vernon and Seymour swung down from their horses to confront him. Vernon cracked his knuckles while Seymour edged his fingers along his gun belt toward his holster, making Oliver slide to a halt.

With a large hand, Hank hauled a rifle sheath to the ground. He flicked it open, but he was surprised to find it contained a four-foot-long metal tube. He tossed the tube in the air, let it turn end-over-end twice, and then caught it.

"Please be careful," Oliver whimpered. "My equipment is important."

Hank rolled the tube between his palms.

"Important as in expensive?"

"No. Important as in easily breakable."

Hank snorted and threw the tube over his shoulder. Oliver dived for the tube, catching it and then juggling it before he held it.

Hank dragged the largest saddlebag to the ground. He reached inside, discarded two books, and drew out a glass circle. He peered through it, the image of his huge eye appearing for a moment, and then flinched back, blinking.

"What's this?"

"A lens."

"Is it expensive?"

Oliver fingered the discarded metal tube. "Will you throw it away if I say no?"

"Yup."

"Then it's expensive."

"I like expensive." Hank thrust the lens into his pocket.

"But you'll never find anyone out here who'll pay to own it."

Hank snorted and then drew the lens from his pocket and threw it aside. It hit the ground and rolled.

Oliver uttered a pained whine and then hurried after the rolling lens. He caught up with it as it spiraled to a standstill on a rock. Using a kerchief to cover his hand, Oliver picked up the lens with his fingertips, ensuring he touched only the sides, and then looked through it at the campfire.

As he breathed a sigh of relief, Hank extracted a wooden contraption that looked like a spider's legs from the saddlebag. He waggled the legs back and forth, his eyes boggling.

"What is all this trash?" he asked.

Oliver slipped the kerchief-clad lens into his pocket and placed his hands on his hips.

"This *trash* is valuable, scientific—"

"Did you say valuable?"

Oliver winced. "I did, but it's only valuable to another scientist, and you won't find many of those out here."

"You might be right, but we have ourselves an adventurous spirit." Hank pointed a wooden leg at Oliver. "So what can I do with this?"

"Nothing that would interest you. But I know one thing for sure; you're not stealing it."

Hank gestured at the barren plains. "Who's going to stop me?"

Oliver pointed at Hank with the metal tube, and then thought better of making a potentially threatening gesture and placed it behind his back.

"Nobody, I guess, but however adventurous you are, you won't find any use for my equipment. It is specialized for the observation of a unique stellar event that is happening in Sundown on the day after tomorrow."

"What unique event?"

"A total eclipse of the sun."

"A total what?"

"It's an event in which . . . Are you interested or are you just baiting me?"

"I'm not baiting you," Hank said, his voice lower and containing a hint that he was intrigued. "I just haven't heard of that before."

"I doubt many people will have heard about it, but they're sure to notice it, and the memory will stay with them for the rest of their lives." Oliver patted his chest. "I, on the other hand, will be engaged in important scientific investigation of this most rare phenomenon."

Hank narrowed his eyes. "Is that rare as in valuable?"

"No," Oliver murmured in exasperation. "That's rare as in happening infrequently."

Hank snorted his breath, and then tugged his gun from its holster.

"You're not being hospitable," he said, aiming the gun at Oliver's chest. "We've given you every chance to be friendly, but you've not taken those chances."

"Don't shoot him yet, Hank," Vernon urged, raising a hand. "I've been thinking. People will pay to see things that are rare."

"That's some mighty fine thinking." Hank turned to Oliver. "So, will people pay to see this rare event?"

"Of course not. The sky will darken like the night. So everyone, whether they know about the eclipse or not, will see it."

"But folks would need to know where it's happening."

"They would. But I can't see ordinary folk traveling into the path of totality . . ." Oliver trailed off when Hank took a long pace forward and pressed the gun up against his temple.

"And?"

Oliver rocked his eyes up to focus on the gun, and then offered a tentative smile.

"And perhaps I wasn't thinking about this hard enough." He took a deep breath. "The eclipse is a unique event and I'm sure that adventurous men such as you gentlemen will find opportunities for personal gain."

"Now I'm beginning to like the sound of it." Hank lowered his gun and gave Oliver a huge slap on the back that knocked him to his knees. "Tell me more."

Chapter Two

With Fergal O'Brien at his side, Randolph McDougal trundled their wagon into Sundown.

It was late in the day and people were bustling as they went about their business. The town consisted of a main drag with buildings on either side. Most were wooden and crudely constructed, but the same couldn't be said about the stone-built complex of the mission and surrounding buildings about which the town had originally formed.

Although the mission might once have been imposing, now it had fallen into near-ruin, with crumbling walls, a chapel with half its roof missing, and many of the buildings around the quadrangle nothing more than heaps of stone.

"I reckon," Randolph said, "we should ask about Maria in the mission, being as how she performs miracles."

"We know how unlikely it is that she does that," Fergal said. "No, a saloon is the best place to ask for information. We'll try the nearest."

He pointed to a saloon opposite the mission, the El Hombre.

"But I have a hunch the mission is the best place to try."

Randolph waited until Fergal started to shake his head, and then drew his attention to a sign swinging above the door to one of the mission's more robust buildings.

"The Mission Santa Maria Saloon," Fergal said, reading aloud. He snorted an appreciative laugh. "That might be a good place to try first, after all."

Randolph veered the wagon toward the mission. On his own wagon, Woody said nothing as he filed in behind, but then again he'd been quiet ever since they'd left Shinbone.

Three months ago, Woody had joined them to present his casket, the Treasure of Saint Woody, as an attraction in Fergal's show. The casket was a closed box that purportedly contained treasure and that, for a dollar a go, people could try to find a way to open and win the treasure.

So far nobody had.

As for the rest of the show, Fergal attempted to sell his universal remedy to cure all ills, a tonic that usually gave its unfortunate victims a bellyache. While Randolph, when he wasn't being miraculously *cured* by Fergal's tonic, busied himself with making items for their display of authentic historical memorabilia. Only this morning he'd painted a plank of wood from the *Mayflower,* although he was now wondering if he'd been wise to plant several bullets in the wood to give it an authentic flavor.

Between them, they made just enough money to survive as they traveled from town to town, provided they left town quickly after Fergal had sold his tonic. Woody had joined them with the promise that his mysterious casket would make them a fortune, but so far, the new addition to their show had done nothing to improve their popularity.

When they reached the mission, Randolph and Fergal jumped down from their wagon and went into the saloon, leaving Woody to look after the wagons.

A smaller sign beside the door said that the owner was Ophelia Green, and when they went inside they found that, aside from Ophelia, who stood behind the bar, the saloon was otherwise unoccupied. Polished chairs surrounded scrubbed tables. The floor was well brushed, making this the neatest and cleanest saloon Randolph had ever seen.

They headed across the room and leaned on the bar. Fergal batted a flurry of trail dust from his sleeves, and then clapped his parched mouth open and closed.

"We want information," he said. "But as we've been on the trail since noon, we sure are thirsty."

Ophelia patted a barrel on the bar and smiled.

"Then I have just the drink for thirsty travelers," she declared.

With a long pull of the pump set into the barrel, she

poured a glassful of thick, slimy liquid, and then presented the glass to Fergal, who eyed it with suspicion and then pushed it along to Randolph.

Randolph took the offered brew and, with the back of his hand, swiped away the layer of froth. He gulped a mouthful.

Years of drinking Fergal's foul-tasting tonic had made him impervious to most bad tastes, but even so, this slimy concoction made his stomach lurch. He slammed the glass back on the bar and spat out the drink in a great fountain across the bar and floor.

"What in tarnation is this foul brew?" he demanded.

Ophelia produced a towel and mopped up Randolph's spit.

"Sarsaparilla."

Randolph scraped his tongue over his teeth, but he failed to free his mouth of the cloying taste.

"Sarspa-what?"

"It's a healthy root derivative. You extract the—"

"I'd be obliged if you'd extract a beer instead."

Ophelia dropped the towel on the bar and favored Randolph with a sympathetic smile.

"I don't serve beer. I run a temperance saloon."

Fergal scratched his forehead. "Then a whiskey will do."

"It wouldn't. As I said, this is a temperance saloon." She narrowed her eyes. "You do know what that means, don't you?"

"This is a saloon," Fergal said, speaking slowly with the tone he employed when dealing with particularly obstructive people. "You tend bar. I want *you* to give *us* a beer, and if you haven't got beer, we want whiskey."

"It doesn't work like that. I *don't* serve beer. I *don't* serve whiskey. I *do* serve sarsaparilla. And if that isn't to your liking, you'll have to brave El Hombre's inappropriate behavior."

Fergal stared at her agog before he shook off his bemusement.

"This is the oddest saloon I've ever been in, but to save us from having to visit this other establishment, I'd welcome some information. We're looking for someone called Maria. I presume the Mission Santa Maria is a good place to start looking."

"Why are you interested in my charge?" Ophelia said, a stern jaw and flaring eyes replacing her previously calm demeanor.

"Your charge?" Fergal murmured, taken aback. "We didn't know that. We just came here to—"

"I know why you came here. You came to stare at her and then go away and tell people she'd made your hair grow or some such nonsense. Well, she doesn't need that kind of attention." She backed away for a pace. "We're going to the evening service shortly, so I'd be obliged if you'd drink up and leave."

Randolph and Fergal glanced at each other, silently noting that they'd been surprised by her harsh words.

"No offense meant," Fergal said, but Ophelia had already turned her back on them.

The two men considered the foaming sarsaparilla. They both shivered, and then headed outside.

"At least we know where Maria will be if you're still interested," Randolph said, as they headed to their wagon, "but it doesn't sound as if she performs miracles."

"As I thought," Fergal said. "But we've come this far . . ."

Randolph nodded, but when they joined Woody, he wasn't as accepting.

"This is a waste of time," he declared. "There is no profit to be had in chasing after a supposed miracle worker."

"I know," Fergal said. "But we don't want any more repetitions of what happened in Shinbone with everyone refusing to buy my tonic because of her. We'll see what we're up against and then move on."

Woody considered the chapel, sneered, and turned to look at El Hombre across the road, which with the sun closing on the distant mountains was attracting a steady stream of people.

"So you are determined to fritter away your life on matters you cannot change, are you?" he said. He jumped down from his wagon. "I prefer to remold the world to my liking."

With that cryptic comment, Woody tipped his stove hat to them and walked off toward El Hombre.

"He's a strange man," Randolph said, as he watched him depart.

Over the last few months, they'd discussed their new associate many times and, accordingly, Fergal firmed his jaw, not wanting to admit he'd made a mistake in letting Woody join them.

"One day he'll make us that fortune he claimed he would. Leave him be."

"But he's creepy."

"He is," Fergal said with a smile. "So it's all the better for us that he's on our side."

Randolph raised his eyebrows, silently conveying that he wasn't sure about that. Then, without further comment, they headed to the chapel.

The building dominated the area, although it didn't have much competition. Around the quadrangle many of the buildings lacked roofs and most lacked more than one wall too.

They picked their way around piles of rubble that might once have been buildings that connected to the chapel. Two furrows scraped a route to the doorway, the meaning of which neither man knew. When they went in through the doorless entrance, they saw that the chapel was as derelict as it appeared from the outside.

Aside from several rows of chairs, the only other furniture was a lopsided altar, the top of it hewn from an irregular slab of flat stone. The sweet smell of decay permeated everything. The walls were mildewed and appeared undecided as to whether they wanted to fall inward or outward. The tops of the walls had outlines that were almost as jagged as the distant mountains.

The building itself had a roof over only half its length, and the roof that was there was latticed and raining down dust as it awaited an opportune moment to join the other half on the floor.

Although the sun was bleeding red rays along the tops of the walls, the only inhabitants were roosting birds, and there was no sign that the promised service was about to begin. With a bemused glance at each other, Fergal and Randolph sat in the front row and waited.

Presently, from behind them, the shuffling of feet sounded along with an intermittent scraping sound.

Randolph turned, expecting to find that the rest of the congregation was arriving, but what he saw took him aback. Ophelia was dragging a bed into the chapel and on it lay a young woman with her hands clasped over her chest.

Randolph jumped to his feet, aiming to help her bring the woman in, but Ophelia shot him a warning glare. Whether that was because of their previous disagreement or because she preferred to deal with the burden herself, Randolph didn't know, but he sat back down.

Ophelia brought the bed to the front of the chapel, turned it round so that the prone woman could see the bulk of the church, and then stood back and lowered her head. Her lips moved, presumably in silent prayer.

Randolph looked at Fergal, who shrugged, and so both men sat quietly, waiting for a suitable time to ask the obvious question.

When Ophelia had finished praying, she took hold of the bed and prepared to maneuver it outside. Fergal raised a hand, halting her.

"We thought there was to be a service," he said.

"There was. That was it." She glared at them, her jaw grinding as if she were fighting to avoid uttering more angry words, but then she softened her expression and spread her hands. When she continued, her tone was kinder. "I'm sorry. That was rude. Everyone is welcome to seek solace here, although the help we can provide is so little. We continue the best we can, but since Father Brown met his unfortunate end, there hasn't been a proper service."

"What happened to him?"

"Three months ago he was shot dead by an unknown gunman." She pointed at a spot before the altar. "I found him lying there one evening. Since then we've kept the mission open as we await a new padre."

"Three months is a long time to wait."

"I know. But Bishop Finnegan is visiting us tomorrow. I hope he will answer our prayers and appoint a new man."

"Our?" Fergal said, peering at the woman on the bed. "I presume you're referring to her, Maria?"

"I am." Ophelia folded her arms and stood back. "You may approach."

Fergal eyed the bed with consternation, noting as Randolph had that the woman on it hadn't moved since she'd been brought here.

"What do you want us to do?" he whispered.

"State your problem. With faith, Maria may be able to help you."

Randolph and Fergal stood and shuffled closer to the bed, both feeling reluctant to speak when faced with such a bizarre situation. Randolph had thought that the young woman was incapacitated or gravely ill, but when they reached the bedside, he saw that she appeared to be asleep.

Maria was around eighteen, but her face was gaunt, marring her otherwise pretty features. Long hair framed her face and lay on the bed to reach beyond her waist. A blanket came up to her chin, but her clothed arms that rested on the top of the blankets suggested she was dressed.

"What's . . . what's wrong with her?" Fergal asked, his voice catching with what sounded like genuine emotion.

"Her story is a sad but inspiring one," Ophelia said, her lecturing tone sounding as if she'd said this many times before. "Two years ago, she was the mission's first novice, and the fact that a young girl called Maria wished to serve at the Mission Santa Maria warmed us all. Then bandits raided the mission on a misguided search for valuables. When Father Brown and I returned, they'd killed the three nuns. Amidst the tragedy, Maria provided a crumb of comfort. She was alive, but an unnoticed injury, or perhaps the shock of what she'd seen, had made her fall into this deep sleep."

"And she's never awoken?"

"No," Ophelia said. "Every day I bring her here to pray that she awakes. She hasn't, but apparently her presence sometimes comforts others."

Randolph caught the skepticism in Ophelia's voice, but only because he'd heard it many times before when people had questioned the effectiveness of Fergal's tonic.

"That's a tragic story," Fergal said. "But I gather you don't think she performs miracles."

"I don't. People come here in distress, and distressed people will often believe anything. I'm pleased she gives them comfort. It shows that good can come from an act of evil, but she doesn't perform miracles." She smiled. "But don't let me dissuade you. What comfort would you like her to provide you?"

Fergal looked at the sleeping Maria, his head cocked to one side. Then he faced Ophelia and smiled.

"I want nothing from her," he said, "but maybe I can do something for her."

Chapter Three

I will not subject Maria to the ministrations of a snake oil seller," Ophelia said, when Fergal had detailed his plan.

Fergal pouted. "I should think not, but do not mistake me for a snake oil seller. I am Fergal O'Brien, the seller of the universal remedy to cure all ills. It cures anything and—"

Ophelia raised a hand. "Do not defile this place of worship with your outlandish claims."

"They are not claims, and I want nothing other than to help her." Fergal spread his hands, revealing his bright green waistcoat, and then reached into his pocket and withdrew a bottle of his tonic. He shook the bottle, making the amber liquid glow despite the gloomy light in the chapel. "I usually charge a dollar, but for her, I'll waive my fee."

She stared at him, snorting her breath, her head beginning to shake.

Randolph moved closer. "If you knew Fergal, you'd know that was a rare offer. Take it."

She favored them both with a brief smile.

"You have good intentions, but I can't risk that you might harm her."

Fergal frowned. "How can I convince you I'll do her no harm?"

She sighed, struggling to find a way to refuse that wouldn't hurt their feelings, but then she raised her eyebrows.

"Fergal O'Brien," she mused. "That's a good Irish name. When Bishop Finnegan arrives tomorrow, would you speak privately with him?"

Fergal gulped. "You mean for a . . . a confession?"

"I do."

"I couldn't possibly." Fergal backed away, while raising his hands in a warding-off gesture.

Ophelia advanced on him with a determined tread that said she'd now found the terms under which she'd let him try to help Maria. Fergal backed away for another pace, knocking into Randolph, who grabbed his shoulders to halt him and then leaned down to speak into his ear.

"Fergal," he urged, "these are good people. Agree you'll confess to this bishop if that's what's needed."

Fergal struggled to remove Randolph's hands, but when he found that he was holding him firmly, he gave a resigned nod to the hopeful-looking woman.

"I'll do as you wish, but warn him that it's been some years since I was last in a confessional."

"How long?"

Fergal considered. "About thirty-three years."

Ophelia peered at him. "And how old are you?"

"Thirty-two."

"How can that be the case?"

"Well, my mother was mighty keen on confessing. I can't be sure, but I reckon about eight months before I was born she'd have—"

"I believe I get the idea," she said.

The sun was dipping toward the horizon when Hank Kelly's group and their new and reluctant associate rode into Sundown.

As they drew up outside El Hombre, Hank glanced at the bank, noting that it was as large and potentially as prosperous as they'd heard.

"Come on," Hank said, glaring at Oliver as he hitched up his horse. "Time to show us why we were right not to kill you."

Oliver grumbled under his breath, but he silenced when Vernon cracked his knuckles.

Hank led the group into El Hombre. He appraised the cold-eyed customers, the battered interior, the broken furniture, and the worrying pile of discolored sawdust by the door.

Only one other customer was at the bar, a black-clad

man wearing a stove hat. He was the only customer not to pay them any attention.

"Are you the owner?" Hank said to the man behind the bar.

"Sure am," the man said. "I'm Sydney Grant. What can I do for you?"

"We'd be obliged," Hank said, with a big smile and pleasant tone, "if you'd spare us a few moments to consider the chance of a lifetime."

Sydney's fixed smile wavered for a moment.

"You have one minute."

Hank pushed Oliver forward. "My associate will explain."

Oliver smoothed his jacket and then stood tall and cleared his throat.

"On the day after tomorrow a rare alignment will occur in which our nearest astronomical body will obscure the solar disc for three minutes and eleven seconds."

Sydney's eyes glazed. He shook himself and blinked twice.

"I have a question: what does *solar* mean?"

"In this case it refers to the sun."

Sydney nodded. "I have a second question. What does *alignment* mean?"

"It means—"

Hank slapped a hand over Oliver's mouth.

"What my associate is trying to convey," he said, "is

the amazing news that the sun will disappear from the sky for three minutes."

Sydney opened his mouth wide and slapped a hand over it.

"I know something even more amazing. Every night the sun disappears from the sky for—"

"This will happen during the day."

Sydney edged to the end of his bar and glanced through the window.

"Can't see the sun now on account of those low clouds."

Hank lowered his head, breathing deeply to get his irritation under control, and then looked up.

"This event doesn't involve clouds or the night. It's because the moon has covered the sun." He glanced at Oliver, who nodded.

Sydney snorted. "The moon doesn't cover the sun."

Oliver coughed and raised a finger. "Whether you believe it or not, this rare event will happen. It is rare because the moon crosses the ecliptic only twice a month while precessing annually by approximately nineteen degrees. This allows only infrequent alignments in any one location."

Sydney nodded. "I have a question."

Hank pushed Oliver out of the way.

"You don't need to know the technical details," he said. "You need only to know that it will happen."

"My question wasn't technical. I want to know what it is you're trying to sell me."

"I'm selling you a once-in-a-lifetime opportunity for your customers to appreciate something wondrous. You could double, triple, perhaps quadruple your saloon income."

"I can appreciate that. But I've been thinking. The thing about the sun is that it's in the sky. And the thing about the sky is that it's up there." Sydney pointed up. "I reckon my customers can look up and see it for themselves. I don't need you."

"Except my good friend knows when this rare event will take place."

"I read a wonderful invention called a newspaper. It's sure to carry details about this event. I still don't need you."

"But you do. My good friend has specialist knowledge that people will pay to acquire."

Sydney rubbed his chin. "And what's the price of this specialist knowledge?"

Hank smiled now that he'd gathered Sydney's interest. He glanced through the saloon's rear door and into the adjoining hotel entrance hall.

"Hospitality in your fine hotel."

"I can spare a room."

Hank placed his face before Sydney's. "And seventy-five percent of your additional income."

"Seventy-five percent!" Sydney spluttered, taking a step backward. "I'll offer five."

Vernon advanced and rocked back his fist, but Hank grabbed his arm.

"Stop making fun of me or I release his arm."

"All right." Sydney smiled. "Ten."

Hank tipped back his hat. "Seventy-four."

"You're no good at negotiating." Sydney waved a dismissive hand at them. "And your minute is up without your getting my interest."

He moved to go, but screeched still when, in a move like lightning, Seymour drew his gun. He raised his hands as Seymour sighted his chest.

"You are going nowhere," Seymour muttered.

"If that was a threat . . ." Sydney considered Seymour's steady gun, then Hank's flaring eyes, and then Vernon's bunched fists. He provided a beaming smile. "Then you three are just the kind of men I'm looking for—but not the babbling one."

Sydney beckoned them to join him in his back room. Seymour and Vernon looked at Hank for guidance; after consideration, he nodded and then glared at Oliver.

"Your eclipse is not so interesting, after all," he said. "So this is where we part company."

Hank patted Oliver on the back, uttered a snort of contempt, and then followed Sydney. The other two favored Oliver with mocking smiles before they too went behind the bar.

Only when Oliver had been left alone did he breathe a sigh of relief. He lowered his head to the bar and rested his forehead on the cool and sticky wood before he sat up.

Then he flinched on finding that the black-clad man who had been at the bar had sidled along to join him, having arrived without making a sound.

"I am Woody," this man said, raising his stove hat. He provided a wide smile that didn't reach his eyes. "Tell me more about this eclipse."

With Ophelia acquiescing now that he had given in to her terms, Fergal stood over Maria.

He gestured to Ophelia to raise the sleeping woman, and then removed the stopper from the bottle of his universal remedy to cure all ills. When Maria was sitting upright, he moved the bottle to her lips. He was still unsure how he'd make her drink, but thankfully Ophelia took the bottle from him.

She sniffed the tonic, and then recoiled, blinking rapidly.

"This smells like . . . like rotting cabbage," she said.

"Actually it smells like a rotting polecat," Randolph said helpfully.

"Nothing that's good for you smells or tastes good," Fergal said, waggling a finger.

"But does it have to smell this rank?"

Fergal set his hands on his hips. "And this from the woman who inflicts sarsaparilla on her customers."

"Sarsaparilla is a healthy—"

"*Healthy* did you say?"

Ophelia and Fergal stared at each other until she nodded, accepting Fergal's point. She sniffed the tonic again, shivered, and then shuffled closer to Maria. Using two fingers, she massaged Maria's throat with one hand while placing the index finger of the other hand into Maria's mouth to open it.

Fergal and Randolph turned away, feeling they shouldn't watch what looked as if it were a private act.

"Is that enough?" Ophelia asked presently.

They turned back to see she was dabbing Maria's mouth with a kerchief while shaking the half-empty bottle with the other.

"For a condition as serious as this," Fergal said, "she should drink the whole bottle."

Ophelia nodded, and continued encouraging Maria to drink until the bottle was empty. Then they stood back and looked at her.

"How long should it take?" Ophelia asked, her voice catching, suggesting that despite the unlikely possibility, she still hoped that the tonic would work.

"The remedy is rapid," Fergal said, his honest-sounding tone making them all lean forward. "She should be coming around any moment . . ."

Fergal raised himself slightly.

Nobody breathed as they stared at the sleeping woman, waiting for something, anything to change. Then with a huge exhalation of breath, Fergal rocked back down on his heels and bowed his head.

"Your tonic to cure all ills does not appear to have worked," Ophelia said in a matter-of-fact manner.

With a look of wide-eyed frustration, Fergal stared at Maria, who was still lying as peacefully as she had been before drinking his tonic. He gripped a hand into a tight fist, and then snatched the empty bottle from Ophelia's grasp and hurled it at the nearest wall. As the shattered glass tinkled to the floor, he turned on his heel and strode from the chapel.

Randolph gave Ophelia an apologetic smile and then followed him outside. He found Fergal sitting on the chapel steps, breaking a stray stalk of grass into segments, and then throwing them to the ground.

"You really hoped it'd work this time, didn't you?" he said, sitting beside him.

"What do you mean by *this time?*" Fergal grumbled. "My universal remedy is a genuine tonic."

Randolph provided a comforting nod. He always found it touching that, despite all the evidence to the contrary, Fergal still believed in the power of his universal remedy.

"Of course it is. And maybe it did her some good that we can't see." Randolph considered the twilight redness on the horizon. "So what with you having a confession with Bishop Finnegan tomorrow, perhaps Ophelia will let you try again before we leave."

Fergal slapped the ground. "I intend to do just that. And I'll keep on trying until I make that young woman wake up."

Randolph moved to give him an encouraging slap on the shoulder, but then stopped when Ophelia came through the doorway behind them.

"You won't," she said. "I let you try the once, but not again."

Fergal stared up at her, his jaw grinding as he considered arguing, before relenting with a sigh.

"I just wish there was something we could do to help."

"There isn't anything you can do for her." She sat down beside Fergal and gestured with a long sweep of her arm, taking in the crumbling mission. "Or for either of us."

"What do you mean?"

"As I said, Bishop Finnegan is coming tomorrow to decide whether the Church will appoint a new padre, but I fear he will conclude that funds are better spent elsewhere. I've run the Mission Saloon for the last three years, but without the Church's support, I won't be able to continue. Then the small progress Father Brown made here will end, and I don't know what will become of myself and Maria."

Fergal considered this information, his eyes alighting with an interest that Randolph had seen many times before, which said his devious mind was starting to work.

"What would Bishop Finnegan need to see to decide to keep the mission going?" he asked.

"He would need to see proof that the town is no longer a dangerous place and that the townsfolk welcomed Father Brown's message," she intoned, as if she were quoting from a letter. "And that he had made progress not only spiritually, but also artistically, culturally, and educationally."

"And how many of those did he succeed with?"

Ophelia raised a hand to her ear, drawing Fergal's attention to the sounds of revelry emanating from El Hombre. The distant crack of a gunshot rent the air, making her smile ironically.

"This is still a lawless town, so despite the hard work Father Brown put in, the answer is none. Sundown is as bereft of education, art, culture, and spiritual thoughts as this mission is of upright walls."

Fergal nodded. Then he slapped his bony knees and stood.

"Don't despair, Ophelia. I am a showman." As a volley of gunshots exploded in the road, along with hoots of merriment from El Hombre, Fergal cast his gaze around the ruined mission. "I may have only one night to prepare, but tomorrow Bishop Finnegan will be so impressed by what he sees here, he won't even notice the mission walls!"

Chapter Four

I can't see how you can help," Randolph said, as he glared at the frothy mass of his sarsaparilla in the Mission Saloon.

"Neither can I yet," Fergal said. He poked his glass around in a circle. "But if I can't make Maria wake up, I will let her keep her home."

"I've never seen you like this before." Randolph leaned toward him. "Tell me the truth. What devious scheme have you got going on in that—?"

"None," Fergal snapped. Then in irritation, he gulped down a mouthful of foam. When he'd stopped coughing and spluttering, he continued. "Just for once I'd like to do something good and help someone."

Randolph looked at Fergal, but when he met his gaze, he nodded. Then both men looked out the window at the El Hombre.

Two men were being thrown out of the saloon, and judging from the gestures the owner was making, it appeared to be for fighting. The men went barreling out into the road where they stumbled into a fight that was already in progress between two other men who were knocking each other back and forth.

The interruption made everyone stop and glare at each other. Then the two fighting men joined forces to take on the two new men.

People spilled out onto the road to shout encouragement to one group or the other, although their display of favoritism initiated a round of shoving and shouting among the spectators as well.

A new brawl started and then spread back into the saloon. A chair and then a table came flying through the already broken window, followed by a man who rolled out, and without breaking his stride, stormed back into the saloon with his fists raised.

"This won't be easy," Randolph murmured, dragging his attention away from the escalating chaos to poke an idle finger into his foaming brew.

Fergal nodded. "It won't, but the situation as I see it is: we haven't got enough time to clean up this town, so we have to make sure that Bishop Finnegan doesn't see any unruly activity going on."

"That means we'll have to keep him in the mission and make sure he sees only what he needs to see: spiritual, cultural, artistic, and educational things," said Randolph, as he considered the small raised area at the back of the saloon. "He's here for only the one night, so perhaps we could cover all the requirements in one go with a show of some kind."

"You're right," Fergal said, brightening as the idea grabbed his imagination. "We'll put on a show for him devoted to cultural pursuits, an evening of refined and sophisticated entertainment."

Both men looked at each other and smiled, acknowledging that neither of them had a clue as to what a night of cultural pursuits entailed, but that that wouldn't stop them trying.

"Ophelia can take care of the spiritual aspect," Randolph said.

"And our display of authentic historical memorabilia will show him that the townsfolk have access to culture. And as for artistic and educational element . . . any ideas?"

Both men sat silently. When his mind remained blank, Randolph looked around the saloon for inspiration. Then he flinched on finding that Woody had returned. He was standing behind them, having approached without making a sound.

"I can resolve your problem," Woody said. He gestured to the man loitering in the doorway. "Let me introduce Oliver Rhinehart, the world's foremost expert on astronomy."

Oliver cast a nervous glance at the escalating brawl outside, and then shuffled toward them.

"I'm not the foremost," he said. "Well, not yet."

"You are the foremost," Woody intoned. "Remember that when you perform."

Oliver gulped and lowered his head, leaving Fergal to ask the obvious question.

"What can he do?"

"Oliver tried to sell an idea to Sydney Grant, the owner of the El Hombre." Gunfire roared outside, and Woody cast a disapproving glance into the road. Three burly men were breaking up the fight with guns and fists. Curiously, they then threw everyone back into the saloon. "He was not interested. He has no ambition beyond stopping the fighting in his saloon so that his customers can spend more time drinking. But I can make Oliver's idea work."

"And what is his idea?"

"Oliver will educate the townsfolk about the greatest moneymaking idea ever to come to Sundown." Woody raised his hat to emphasize his delight. "I give you, astronomy!"

Hank Kelly looked out of the hotel room window on the first floor of El Hombre.

Despite the poor light, from his elevated position he had a good view of the bank farther down the road and could see through the large window almost to the back wall. The only protection he'd seen was a metal grill stretching from the counter to the ceiling.

With the back of his hand, he patted Vernon's chest.

"This location is perfect," he said.

"Yeah," Vernon said. "That bank is mighty tempting."

"Not only the bank," Seymour said. "Did you see Sydney's safe in his back room?"

Everyone nodded while chuckling with delight.

"And we're in comfort," Vernon said. "All we have to do is bang heads together while we pick the easiest way to get rich. Life don't get no better than this."

The three men chortled happily, and then left their room and headed down the stairs.

They stopped in the saloon and cast surly glares at the customers, ensuring nobody was taking exception to them after they'd broken up the fight earlier, but no one met their eyes. So they headed to the hotel's dining room, where they found Sydney Grant sitting at the head table hunched over a ledger.

"Any sign of that fight breaking out again?" Sydney asked without looking up.

"We picked out the ringleaders and Vernon impressed your annoyance upon them." Hank patted Vernon's back. "So while they still have the impression of his fist on their faces, they won't cause no more trouble."

Sydney totaled up a column of figures and grunted with pleasure.

"Good, and how are the preparations for Bishop Finnegan's visit tomorrow going?"

"We don't know nothing about that," Hank said. "You never told us that you—"

"Your job is not to wait for me to tell you what to do, but to anticipate what will concern me. And from overheard information that has been passed on to me, I gather that your former associate has gone to the Mission Saloon where he will perform a lecture before Bishop Finnegan. If he is successful, he will attract customers away from El Hombre."

"Oliver is the most boring man I've ever met. He won't say nothing that'll interest anyone." Hank thought back to what he'd seen upstairs. "But when we were watching the . . . when we were looking out the window, we saw the Mission Saloon. It was nearly deserted."

"As it should be." Sydney looked up for the first time and fixed Hank with his firm gaze. "But if people go in there, I expect you to ensure they choose a different saloon to frequent."

Hank nodded. "I understand."

"I didn't employ you to understand, but in this case . . ." Sydney stood and beckoned them to join him at the window. "I presume you've seen the mission?"

"You can't miss the chapel," Hank said, looking at the large complex. "It's the largest building in town."

"It is. Admittedly the mission is not looking its best right now, but all that will change when it becomes mine. From what I hear, after the recent unfortunate deaths, the Church is set to abandon it." Sydney snorted a laugh, his smirk suggesting he knew more about what had happened than was commonly known. "That'll let me buy it cheaply. Then, when I've restored it to its former glory, it will make a fine home for me, and a fine saloon for my customers."

Sydney raised his eyebrows, inviting a response.

"We'll make sure you get what you want."

Sydney clapped his hands and then shooed them away toward the door.

"Then make sure that you do. Nothing must stand in my way."

Chapter Five

Bishop Finnegan is no fool," Ophelia said. "I can't see how one night of carefully staged presentations will convince him that Sundown is a safe place for the mission when the raucous proof that it isn't is going on in El Hombre across the road."

"I am a showman," Fergal said, looping his hands into his jacket lapels and puffing out his chest proudly. "Making people believe in the impossible is my job."

Ophelia narrowed her eyes. "You mean like convincing me that your tonic would wake Maria?"

Fergal set his hands on his hips. "My tonic is a genuine product. No injury is so bad, no ailment . . ."

Prior to this diversion, the morning meeting in the Mission Saloon to finalize today's arrangements had been progressing well.

Bishop Finnegan would arrive by train in Shinbone in the early afternoon. The long journey to Sundown meant there would be only enough time for a quick tour of the town before nightfall.

Hopefully, the usual rowdy behavior in El Hombre wouldn't have erupted by then. For the rest of the evening, they would distract him from seeing anything unsavory with a night of refined entertainment.

Finnegan himself would conduct a service in the chapel. This would be followed by a trip around Randolph's display of authentic historical memorabilia, with emphasis on the religious relics. Then the night would culminate with Oliver's educational lecture on the eclipse in the Mission Saloon where Ophelia would ensure there was a ready supply of healthy sarsaparillas.

Fergal hoped this would convince Finnegan that even if the artistic element was lacking, the mission was catering to the town's spiritual, cultural, and educational needs. The nods everyone provided confirmed that the others agreed, but this good cheer didn't extend to Ophelia.

"The merits of your tonic are irrelevant," she said. "I still fail to see why a dry lecture on the sky will impress the bishop."

"It will not be dry," Fergal said. "I've already discussed the need to be entertaining with Oliver."

Fergal gestured to Oliver, and the scientist stepped forward, nodding eagerly.

"He has. I will start with an explanation of the solar eclipse and build to a stunning finale where I will bring the night sky inside." Oliver frowned. "Although to bring the finale to life I will need help from a practical person."

The mention of him needing help silenced everyone. Woody was the first to react.

"In that case," he said, standing, "I will volunteer to go to Shinbone to collect Bishop Finnegan."

"And I'll volunteer to go with you," Fergal said, after a moment's thought.

Randolph, who up until now hadn't taken part in the discussion, glanced at each man in turn, and then gave a rueful sigh.

"In which case," he said, with a resigned tone, "I'll volunteer to stay and do all the hard work."

Bishop Finnegan's train was late.

So Fergal jumped down from the buggy he'd borrowed from Ophelia and left Woody to his own business.

Bearing in mind his previous disastrous visit to Shinbone, he didn't want to risk being seen by the people who had been unimpressed by his tonic. So he headed into Milton's Saloon, the quietest and cleanest-looking saloon on the main road.

At the bar, a man was reading one of the provided newspapers, but no other customers were inside other than a snoring man in the corner. Strangely, the saloon provided entertainment. On a stage at the back of the saloon, a tights-clad man was emoting with a sword thrust out.

"Verily and forsooth, thou are more irksome than a knave's jackass," the tights-clad man appeared to say, although Fergal wasn't sure of the exact words, as the man was droning on in a language that he barely recognized as being English. The man rubbed a finger along his thin moustache and grinned, as if he'd said something witty, before continuing. "But lo, what be . . . ?"

Fergal blocked out the rest of the speech. On the bar, a card depicted the tights-clad man brandishing a sword, advertising him as THADDEUS T. THACKENBACKER THE THIRD, THE WEST'S GREATEST LIVING THESPIAN.

Fergal wavered between finding another saloon or suffering the bellowing in the background, and then shrugged and ordered a whiskey, but the barkeep, Milton, had rested his head on his arms and was delivering rasping snores.

Even Fergal's fist slamming on the bar failed to raise him from his deep slumbers. So he poured himself a glass of whiskey, threw a dime on the counter, and picked up a spare newspaper.

After five minutes of rustling through the print, he found the article he was looking for.

He raised his eyebrows and leaned closer to the newspaper. A chuckle escaped his lips, making the other reader at the bar look over his shoulder to see what had amused him.

"What's an eclipse?" he asked.

"It's when the sun disappears from the sky," Fergal said.

"That happens every night."

"I know. But this happens during the day—and it doesn't involve clouds either."

The man shrugged. "That doesn't sound exciting. When's it happening?"

"Tomorrow."

"Where's it happening?"

Fergal just smiled, folded the newspaper, and placed it back on the bar.

Presently, the emoting from the back of the saloon ended, and Thaddeus strode to the front of the stage. Bright afternoon sunlight illuminated the rows of empty tables as, with a tights-clad leg held straight and thrust out before the other, Thaddeus bowed deeply.

"And that concludes my simple tale," he proclaimed, his voice booming in the near-deserted room, "told by your humble strolling player."

Fergal knocked back his whiskey and pushed the glass along the bar to Milton. The glass nudged his arm, waking him.

Milton rubbed his eyes and stifled a yawn. On seeing Thaddeus standing bowed and silent on the stage, he placed his hands together ready to clap. Then he thought better of it and polished the glass instead.

Fergal, exchanging a wink and a bemused sigh with Milton, headed to the door.

He had a hand on the swinging doors when the thought tapped at his mind that they didn't have an artistic element for tonight's show, so he turned and made his way past the empty tables to the stage. He tipped his hat to Thaddeus.

"What can I do for you?" Thaddeus boomed, standing tall as he peered down at Fergal.

Fergal considered him, taking in his tights, his gaudy clothes, his gleaming sword.

"You're an actor, are you?"

"I am but a humble purveyor in the arts and crafts of that wondrous joy that is the theater." As Fergal scratched his head, Thaddeus leaned forward. "Yes, I am an actor."

"Are you any good at it?"

"Did you not see my performance?"

"I only suffered . . . saw the last ten minutes."

"Then you will have missed my majestic staging," Thaddeus intoned, his voice echoing. "*Romeo and Juliet* is a tragic love story that speaks to us from down the ages."

Fergal snorted. "Pity you had to speak it so loudly. It's hard to enjoy your whiskey when the glass is rattling."

"An actor never sullies his performance with poor enunciation." Thaddeus thrust his sword aloft. "As a result, my one-man show is legendary."

Fergal glanced around the saloon. "Perhaps it is, but I didn't realize a one-man show referred to the size of the audience."

Thaddeus sneered. "You obviously can't count. Five people are here this afternoon."

"Yeah, me, you, Milton, a man reading a newspaper,

and that snoring whiskey-hound in the corner." Fergal looked Thaddeus up and down. "Your notice says you're doing a second performance tonight. So, do you know how to use that sword?"

"Why?"

"Because at night in a town like Shinbone, a man wearing those tights had better have some protection."

With a flourish, Thaddeus dug the point of his sword into the stage and leaned on it to glare down at Fergal, his chin jutting.

"Why are you sneering at the West's greatest living thespian?"

"I'm not. But I do have a proposition for you. Shinbone obviously isn't sophisticated enough to appreciate your talents."

Thaddeus' shoulders slumped. "You are so right."

"But I'm returning to Sundown. That town's right sophisticated. They'll appreciate seeing something artistic."

"Perhaps." Thaddeus stood and waved a dismissive hand at Fergal. "But I have a booking here. I couldn't possibly disappoint my adoring public."

Fergal glanced over his shoulder at the bar where the newspaper reader had left and Milton had resumed his slumbers. Then he looked at the other sleeping man, who was snoring even louder than before.

"I reckon nobody would notice if you left."

"Either way, I am a man of honor." Thaddeus drew his

sword from the wood and paced to the back of the stage. "I will not leave until I have fulfilled my obligations."

Fergal sighed. "That'll disappoint Ophelia. She'd love to stage your performance in her saloon."

Thaddeus turned back, his eyes wide and lively. He ran a finger along his moustache, ending with an extra flourish.

"A woman, you say?"

"Do you know what Oliver will do with these?" Randolph asked.

"I don't," Ophelia said. "I'm just concentrating on completing the task at hand."

Randolph took the hint and resumed his work. Between them sat a heap of wooden slats along with a pile of thirty pieces of black cloth, each four feet square.

For the last two hours he'd been making the slats into squares. So far he had completed fifteen. He had also made a slightly larger square out of four chunkier lengths of wood.

When he'd completed a square, he passed it to Ophelia and she stretched the black cloth over the wood and then tacked the cloth in place. The work was monotonous. But Randolph reckoned that sitting cross-legged on the floor of a room behind the saloon with Ophelia and the sleeping Maria was a soothing way to pass the afternoon when compared to his usual hectic activities with Fergal.

He finished the latest square and placed it on top of the pile of unused shapes beside Ophelia, and then took the opportunity to stand and stretch. He wandered closer to Maria.

She was lying as she had done last night in her bed, with her arms above the blankets and her long hair framing her face, still looking as if she was sleeping. The only noise she made was her breath wheezing in and out.

"Does she ever appear to notice you when you're working nearby?" he asked.

Ophelia broke off from work on her current cloth and sighed. When she spoke her voice was low.

"I never talk about her in such an offhand manner. I presume she can hear and so I behave accordingly."

"I'm sorry." Randolph sat back down and picked up the next slat.

Ophelia looked up from her work to consider him.

"I know you mean well, and to answer your question, I see small signs that she is listening, things others don't see, such as her not liking loud noises." She raised her voice slightly. "We're halfway through, Maria. When we're finished we'll eat."

"That'll be fine, Ophelia," Randolph said. He turned to Maria and raised his voice. "It's a nice day, Maria, and we can go for a walk later if you want. That'd be nice, wouldn't it, Maria?"

He waited for an answer he knew he wouldn't get, and then turned back to find Ophelia was frowning.

"That was better," she whispered, "but you went too far the other way."

"Sorry." Randolph coughed. "If you don't mind me asking, what will happen to you and Maria if Bishop Finnegan refuses to appoint a new padre?"

"I don't know. I don't earn enough from the sarsaparillas to keep us both. I don't know. I really don't." She put down a completed square of cloth. "That's why I've been so tetchy. The thought that we could be the last people to serve here has tested my faith to the utmost. I'm sorry."

"You have nothing to apologize about. And the bishop must be a good man. Whatever he decides, I'm sure he won't let Maria suffer."

"I know." She grabbed the latest square, but she did so with haste and the wood snapped. She stared at the broken wood and then let out a sob. "Not that it'll matter for long."

Randolph moved to comfort her, but then stopped himself. He stayed crouched with his hands thrust out, wondering if it would be appropriate to put an arm around her shoulders, and then converted the movement into taking the wooden square from her instead. He sat back down and removed the broken slat.

"What do you mean?"

His matter-of-fact manner helped to calm her, and she again lowered her voice so that Maria wouldn't be able to hear.

"She's been like this for two years. The last time I could afford a sawbones, he said she wouldn't survive in this state for even that long, and I can see why. She's wasting away. Another month, perhaps two, and if she doesn't awake, she'll . . ."

She broke off to stifle another sob and then concentrated on tacking cloth onto the latest square.

"Don't worry," Randolph said, offering a comforting smile. "You were right to put your faith in Fergal. He'll impress Bishop Finnegan so much he'll probably appoint himself as the new padre!"

Chapter Six

How much longer do I have to tolerate this infernal heat and these cramped conditions?" Bishop Finnegan demanded.

Fergal glanced over his shoulder from the seat of the buggy. They were only a mile out of Shinbone, and Sundown was still several hours away, but he bit back his original retort to this latest complaint and smiled.

"We're nearly there, Bishop," he said. "I mean, your Grace, your gracious Bishop."

"I am an informal man. Your Excellency will suffice."

"And has Your Excellency enjoyed what he has seen so far?"

"I have not. The train was slow and stifling. Shinbone was filled with the spawn of Satan. I only hope Sundown is more suitable." Finnegan roved his disapproving gaze away from the terrain to consider the strapped-down barrel that was filling the space between him and Thaddeus. "And what is this infuriating object doing here?"

54

"Provisions for the needy," Fergal said, turning to the front before the bishop could lodge any more complaints. He waited until Finnegan had been silent for several seconds, and then leaned toward Woody. "But I could ask you the same question."

"You could," Woody said, looking straight ahead. "I have an idea that will raise interest in tonight's evening of culture pursuits."

Fergal edged closer to Woody and lowered his voice to ensure they weren't overheard.

"An idea involving a barrel of rye whiskey, when we're attempting to please an influential man in a temperance saloon?"

"Temperance does not attract customers away from the rowdy denizens of El Hombre. Whiskey will."

"It will not, because Ophelia will not be serving liquor."

Woody turned up the corners of his mouth with an icy smile.

"We formed a partnership to make a fortune. Your woeful lack of ambition will not stop me."

"It will. There are two of us and only one of you. Randolph will agree with me that we won't do anything to jeopardize Ophelia's attempt to keep the mission open."

Woody glared at Fergal. Then he slapped a firm hand down on his arm.

"I understand. You do not trust me or my ideas." Woody paused, but Fergal couldn't think of an appropriate retort.

"So when we return, I will prove my worth. An empty chapel for the service tonight is unlikely to satisfy Bishop Finnegan. I will fill it."

After pouring cold water on Woody's previous idea, Fergal felt he shouldn't ask for more details about how he would do this, and so he nodded. With that matter concluded, he still had the problem of the barrel intriguing the inquisitive bishop, but that resolved itself when Finnegan broke his brief silence.

"Would it be too much to ask," he demanded, "for you to avoid at least one hole on this journey?"

Fergal sighed, and then drew back on the reins.

"I'll sit in the back and guard the barrel," he said to Woody. "You take the reins."

When Fergal had stopped the horses, he invited Finnegan to join Woody up front. As expected, the bishop wasted no time in jumping down from the buggy and finding a new reason to complain.

"I hope it's more comfortable up there," he grumbled as he passed Fergal.

"I'm sure you'll find the seat more to your liking," Fergal said, with a short bow and an ingratiating smile as he passed.

Finnegan stopped. "Then why didn't you let me sit there from the start, instead of forcing me to suffer endless hours of torment cramped up beside that rank-smelling barrel and that grinning imbecile?"

Fergal reckoned that no answer would satisfy His Excellency, and so he limited himself to gripping his hands into tight fists behind his back, and then climbing up onto the back of the buggy to join Thaddeus.

When they got moving, Fergal peered at Thaddeus over the barrel.

"What will you be performing tonight?" he asked, more to take his mind off his irritating disagreements with Finnegan and Woody than out of any actual interest.

"I perform *Romeo and Juliet*," Thaddeus announced in a booming voice.

"Is it any good?"

"It is Shakespeare." When Fergal looked nonplussed, Thaddeus slammed a fist on the barrel top, raising a sloshing noise from within and a rising plume of rye fumes. "A great play by the greatest playwright in all history. What would you think?"

"Got plenty of gunfights in it, then?"

Thaddeus furrowed his brow. "There is no gunplay in Shakespeare. *Romeo and Juliet* is set in fifteenth-century Verona."

"Where's that?"

"The place is not important. The time is. There were no guns in fifteenth-century Verona, so the action is appropriate to the time." Thaddeus mimed cutting and parrying. "There are sword fights aplenty."

"That explains why you didn't get an audience back

in Shinbone. Men like to hear about gunplay. So what's this play about?"

"It is a tale of two feuding families."

"Ranchers, are they?"

Thaddeus winced. "No. But when the son of one family and the daughter of the other fall in love, the resulting tragedy rips both families apart."

Fergal tapped his chin as he remembered his earlier discussion with Oliver. Urging him to make his lecture entertaining appeared to have spurred him into making a positive change. So after seeing Thaddeus' unpopular performance in Shinbone, he wondered if he could do the same here.

"If you were to put some gunplay in," he said, leaning forward to place his hands on the barrel, "you'll get more men interested."

"I will not rewrite Shakespeare to make some cheap, tawdry entertainment." Thaddeus stroked his moustache with an extravagant gesture.

"But we need to attract more people than you did in Shinbone or this booking will last for even less time than that one did."

Thaddeus winced. "When you put it that way, I can see your point. I will deign to consider suggestions, but I will not remove the sword fights."

Fergal rubbed his chin, considering. "You could make the feuding families ranchers. People might care about them then."

"No." Thaddeus leaned over the barrel to place a heavy hand on Fergal's arm. "Anything more?"

"You could change those funny words into English."

Thaddeus tightened his grip, his eyes flaring.

"And you, a mere showman, presume to better the English of Shakespeare?"

Fergal nodded. "Before we get back to Sundown I reckon I could knock something up that's better than his nonsense."

"Nonsense! Nonsense?" With an angry thrust of his arm Thaddeus rummaged in his pocket and extracted a sheet of paper and a pencil. He slammed them on the barrel. "Go on. Do your worst."

Fergal took the pencil, pondered, and then while timing his scribbling to the swaying of the buggy, he wrote a few words.

He read his writing, changed a word, and then looked up to face the glaring Thaddeus. With his back straight, he placed a hand on his chest and held the other aloft, adopting the required pose of an actor.

"Verona's peaceful," Fergal intoned, "perhaps too peaceful."

Thaddeus whistled through his teeth, his previous irate gaze softening.

"I reckon," he said, "that's nearly a great line."

It was late afternoon when Randolph and Ophelia finished making the squares of black cloth.

While Ophelia went outside to await Bishop Finnegan, Randolph gathered them up and took them to the building beside the stables where Oliver had set up residence.

The scientist was kneeling on the ground, hunched over his work. He had laid out several books and was drawing in such an intense manner that he barely acknowledged Randolph's presence.

Randolph cast him an amused smile and then took a steady stroll around the quadrangle. When he reached the main drag, he saw that the buggy ferrying the bishop was heading into town.

Ophelia was standing before her saloon, nervously rocking from side to side, and so Randolph went over to join her as the welcoming committee.

Woody was sitting in front with the bishop, while Fergal and another man were in the back. When Woody drew the wagon to a halt, he and Fergal stayed on the buggy to let Ophelia take the lead.

"Shall I escort you around the mission, Your Excellency?" she said.

Finnegan got down from the buggy, and then glared at the crumbling mission with disapproval. He turned a full circle, and although the buggy was situated in the right position to block his view of El Hombre, he still sneered.

"I will delay that odious duty for now," he said. "I wish to see the town first, before my tired and battered bones seize up completely."

"It will have to be a brief tour, as we hope you will grace us with a service this evening," Ophelia said. "Then we have planned a sophisticated evening of culture to show you the progress Father Brown made here."

"I suppose I can tolerate that if I must." Finnegan clapped his hands together and set off, not allowing any room for debate. "So let's get this formality over with."

Despite that distinctly unpromising opening statement of intent, Fergal put his plan into operation.

Ophelia returned to her saloon, followed by the new man who had returned with the buggy. Then Woody took the buggy to the stables, while Fergal hurried on to accompany Finnegan, directing him to walk down the quietest side of the road.

Randolph walked along behind, looking out for any signs of trouble that might interrupt their peaceful journey. But they passed the bank and the mercantile to reach the end of the road without incident. Then Finnegan moved to walk along the other side.

Even if Fergal were to steer him on a diagonal route back toward the mission, he would have to pass El Hombre. So Randolph looked to the saloon to see if it was quiet. Unfortunately, at that moment, a roar of anger sounded. Then a man reeled out through the swinging doors and landed in a crumpled heap in the road.

The man lay on the ground, looking as if he wouldn't get up. But then he staggered to his feet, set his feet wide apart in a belligerent stance, and with a roll of his shoulders and his fists held high, he barged back into the saloon.

Randolph could see that before long trouble of the kind that had erupted last night would build up and probably spill out into the road. He glanced at Fergal for guidance.

With a few gestured instructions behind Finnegan's back, Fergal gave Randolph the order that he'd try to delay the bishop's progress, while Randolph quieted things down in the saloon.

Randolph hurried to El Hombre, hearing oaths and cries of pain, along with the crash of chairs hitting the walls. Once inside, he was relieved to see that only two people were engaged in this particular fight, and the man who had fallen outside was near to admitting defeat. He was facing a thickset man who was administering a pummeling that was knocking him toward the door with every blow. Randolph recognized the assailant as being Seymour Cook, one of the men who had arrived with Oliver.

After a flurry of blows, Seymour delivered a swinging punch to the man's face that sent him reeling to the floor. The man lay still groaning. Then he levered himself up with one arm, but he couldn't summon the energy to stand and flopped back down again.

"Get to your feet, Tucker," Seymour muttered, standing over him.

"I can't," Tucker murmured through bloodied lips.

"Then I'll get you some help." Seymour looked over

his shoulder. "Hey, Vernon, hold him up while I finish teaching him a lesson."

Vernon left his seat at the bar, and with determined paces, he joined them and dragged the fallen man to his feet.

Seymour drew back his fist, ready to continue the beating, but that sight was enough for Randolph.

"Release him," he said in a commanding tone.

Seymour kept his fist held back, and then slowly lowered it, and with Vernon, he swung round to face him.

They looked him up and down. Grins appeared on both men's faces as they contemplated the likely continuation of the fight. Then Vernon withdrew his hands to let Tucker fall to the floor with a thud and a groan.

"You reckon I shouldn't have dropped him?" Vernon said, smirking.

Randolph sighed, seeing no way to avoid a fight. He reckoned he still had a few minutes before Finnegan reached the saloon, so he raised his fists.

"Ask me that question again when I've finished with you," he said.

"Can I help you?" Ophelia said from the bar.

"I hope so," a booming voice announced from the doorway.

"Then perhaps you'd like to partake of the house specialty." She bustled a glass onto the bar and gave it a quick sparkle with her apron.

Thaddeus stalked across the room, his gait light. He bowed and then thrust out a hand and, in response, Ophelia held out her hand for him to take it and brush his lips across the fingers.

"The house specialty sounds fine," he said, "but only if it is served by this fair hand, and by the fair maiden to whom it is attached."

Ophelia poured a sarsaparilla. "And which fair gentleman do I have the pleasure of serving?"

"Thaddeus T. Thackenbacker the Third, thespian, gentleman." Thaddeus fingered his moustache. "To name just two of my attributes."

"And why has an actor come to Sundown?"

Thaddeus sipped his drink. His eyes widened for a brief moment. Then he placed the glass on the bar and provided a winning smile.

"I am but a strolling player. I rove wherever the fancy takes me, searching for fair maidens who will patronize my craft." Thaddeus glanced around. "And this could be such an establishment. A saloon owned by a maiden with the entrancing name of Ophelia Green."

Ophelia flushed. "And what do you perform?"

"My highly original performance of *Romeo and Juliet*." Thaddeus handed Ophelia his card.

Ophelia tapped the card. "This claims you're a one-man show."

"I play all forty-one speaking parts. My sword-fighting scenes are a sight to behold." Thaddeus made a wild slash with an imaginary sword. "Cuts and lunges are what my adoring public love to see."

"And will you be wearing these tights when you perform your cuts and lunges?"

"I will."

Ophelia wafted her face with the card. "Then you're hired."

Seymour stepped forward and delivered a wild round-arm punch at Randolph's face. Randolph ducked beneath it. Then, with Seymour's chest unguarded, Randolph swung in a short-armed jab to his belly that made the air blast from his lungs with a bellowing cough.

As Seymour doubled over, Randolph chopped both hands down on the back of his neck, knocking him to his knees, and then tipped him over with a contemptuous push of a boot.

Then he faced Vernon.

This man had been standing back, watching how his tired colleague fared, and despite seeing him knocked to the floor, he smiled with confidence and beckoned Randolph on.

With time pressing, Randolph moved in. He feinted with his right fist, and then the left, both aimed blows making Vernon jerk away, but when Randolph repeated the movements, his assailant became used to the rhythm and didn't move so far.

So for his fifth blow, Randolph followed through.

This time Vernon didn't move out of the way, but when Randolph's fist connected with his cheek, he sure moved. His feet left the floor. He went flying through the air before he landed on his belly. Unable to stop himself, Vernon went skidding across the grimy saloon floor to crash into a table and send its occupants tumbling to the floor.

By the time he'd extricated himself from the mess, Vernon's face was bright red. He stood, batted his hands together, and then, without caution, he charged Randolph.

With his feet planted firmly, Randolph waited to repel his onslaught. But when Vernon reached him, he danced aside with a level of grace for such a big man that would have surprised Vernon if he wasn't busy trying to avoid running into the bar. He failed and bent double over the rim, his chin jerking down to crash into the wood.

He grunted with pain and then straightened, but when he turned, he was unsteady. By now, Seymour was getting to his feet and, after exchanging a look, they stormed in together.

Randolph moved to take on Seymour first, and he wasted no time in bundling him to the floor with a firm punch to the cheek. But while Randolph was lunging forward with the force of his follow-through, Vernon got in a blow of his own. A solid punch to the jaw sent Randolph reeling into the bar.

He stood leaning over the bar, catching his breath, while listening to Vernon move up on him from behind.

He waited until the last possible moment. Then with a deft motion, he danced to the side and jerked his arms up to catch Vernon's head in a headlock.

Vernon squirmed, trying to wrap his arms around Randolph's chest in a bear hug, but he struggled to get a firm grip. Before he succeeded, Randolph clunked Vernon's head on the bar. His forehead landed with a satisfying thud and, without making a sound, Vernon collapsed to the floor.

Randolph checked that Seymour was still down, groaning, and that Finnegan was still not visible through the window. He batted his hands together and moved for the door, but he'd managed only a single pace when a strident voice barked out from behind.

"That's far enough!"

He turned to see the third member of this trio of troublemakers, Hank Kelly. He was standing five feet from the bar and, unlike the previous two men who had been prepared to settle their differences with fists alone, Hank's hand was dangling beside his holster.

"There's no reason for us to trade lead," Randolph said. He offered a smile. "I only came here to ask everyone to be quiet."

Hank returned a sneer. "You should have stayed in the mission. You're not welcome here."

"I don't have to do nothing you—" Randolph broke off, when a hand nudged him from behind.

He started to turn, but he was already too late.

The barkeep Sydney Grant had leaned over the bar and torn Randolph's gun from its holster. Sydney then threw the gun away and Randolph could do nothing but watch it slide to a halt before the door.

"You sure do," Hank said, eyeing the gun lying twenty feet away, smiling for the first time. "You can go for your gun whenever you choose."

Randolph considered the weapon, judging that it was too far away to reach quickly. Then he looked at Hank, seeing no hope of mercy in his cold gaze. So he stood tall and decided to do the only thing he could do: walk to the door and hope Hank wouldn't shoot an unarmed man in the back in cold blood.

He'd started to turn when that hope died. Hank threw his hand to his holster. The gun came to hand in an instant. But then he stilled the motion.

Randolph considered Hank's posture of standing poised, ready to swing the gun up and fire, but long moments passed without him moving. Someone had stopped him from firing, Randolph concluded, but when he looked around the saloon to see who it had been, to his surprise that man was Fergal.

Fergal had come in, picked up Randolph's gun, and had now turned the weapon on Hank.

"Drop that gun and raise that hand," Fergal said, "or I'll tear you in two."

"Try it," Sydney said before Hank could respond, while

swinging a rifle into view from under the bar, "and it'll be the last thing you do."

While Fergal darted his gaze from Sydney to Hank and then back again, facing an impossible dilemma, Hank glared at Fergal, looking as if he'd test his ability to shoot him from the doorway. Fergal already had his gun trained on him, but Randolph was familiar with Fergal's poor gun skills and the outcome was by no means certain.

Randolph hoped Hank wouldn't be able to detect Fergal's lack of skill. So he breathed a sigh of relief when, with a snort, as if he'd chosen to relent rather than being forced to, Hank let the gun drop back into its holster. Then he headed to the bar where he knelt beside the sprawling Vernon and checked on him.

Randolph reckoned this was a good time to beat a retreat. So without a backward glance, he joined Fergal. Together they slipped outside. When they were out on the boardwalk, Fergal breathed his own sigh of relief. Then with a shaking hand, he returned Randolph's gun.

"Obliged," Randolph said, giving Fergal a huge slap on the back.

"I'd be even more obliged," Fergal said, his voice shaking, "if I never have to do that again."

"I'll try to avoid it." He looked around. "Where's Bishop Finnegan?"

"Thankfully he passed the saloon without looking in

and went off in search of things to complain about in the mission, and so missed the things to complain about here."

"Luckily you didn't go with him." Randolph glanced at the gun. "And it's even luckier that Hank didn't test your aim."

"I haven't got an aim. I was more likely to hit my own foot than him."

Randolph leaned toward him. "So we can both be grateful he didn't test who does the thinking between us and who does the shooting."

Fergal laughed. "Yeah. I dread to think what would happen if we ever found ourselves in a situation where we have to rely on me using a gun and you using your brain."

Chapter Seven

Shouldn't I wait until everyone's here?" Bishop Finnegan asked when Ophelia bade him to begin the service.

Ophelia winced. "Everyone *is* here."

Then, before Finnegan could ask any more awkward questions, she busied herself with rearranging Maria's top blanket.

In truth, more people were here than usual, with Fergal and Randolph present, along with Oliver Rhinehart and Thaddeus T. Thackenbacker, and they were trying to compensate for the almost deserted chapel by looking attentive. They didn't need to feign their expressions when Finnegan moved over to stand by Maria.

"I have heard much about you," he said, using a gentle tone for the first time and sounding as if he were talking to someone who could hear him.

"I'm sure your presence will give her great comfort," Ophelia said, when a suitable amount of time had passed to confirm Maria wouldn't answer.

71

"As will your service," Fergal said helpfully.

Finnegan shot Fergal an irritated glare, and then looked to the door, clearly wondering if anyone else would arrive. For several minutes he stood with his arms folded and foot tapping an insistent rhythm on the floor, but when the chapel resolutely refused to fill up, he sighed.

"And it would appear," he said, "that giving this *one* person comfort is all I can hope to achieve here."

"Not one," Fergal said, gesturing to draw Finnegan's attention to himself, and then pointing along the front row. "None of us have missed a single service since we arrived here, and you'll be hearing my confession afterward."

Fergal offered a hopeful smile, but the opportunity to hear thirty-two years of accumulated misdemeanors didn't cheer the disgruntled bishop.

Randolph leaned in toward Fergal. "You'd better make that confession a good one," he whispered, "or we'll fail the first of the requirements."

"Have faith," Fergal said. Then he raised a hand to his ear.

Randolph listened and presently discerned footfalls approaching the chapel. The man whom Seymour had beaten earlier, Tucker Moorhead, edged a tentative and cautious pace into the chapel.

"Come in, come in," Finnegan bade, beckoning him on. "Everyone is welcome."

Tucker removed his hat and crumpled it before him. Then he speeded up, but it wasn't from an eagerness to attend the service. He was being pushed onward by the press of people from behind.

"How did you get these people to come?" Randolph whispered.

"Woody persuaded them," Fergal said, and raised his eyebrows, waiting for Randolph to admit he'd misjudged him, but Randolph just shook his head.

"Then this is sure to go wrong," he grumbled, but despite his gloomy prediction the new people filed in to fill every seat, sitting quietly and respectfully, waiting for the service to start.

For the first time since he'd arrived, Bishop Finnegan smiled.

While Bishop Finnegan's strident tones rose up from the roofless chapel, Seymour Cook and Vernon Black sneaked into the Mission Saloon to see what Randolph and Ophelia had been making earlier.

"If Sydney's right," Vernon said, "Oliver has put together something spectacular to impress the bishop tonight."

Seymour nodded. "So we have to make sure it doesn't."

Vernon felt his tender jaw. "It'll be good to wipe those smiles off Fergal's and Randolph's faces, before we wipe them off permanently."

Seymour grunted that he agreed. Then they headed across the deserted room to the stage. Lying beside it was the only clue to what Oliver would be presenting tonight: a pile of black cloth cut into squares and tacked to slats.

"Any ideas?" Seymour asked.

Vernon rummaged through the pile, finding that although it appeared new, the cloth was holed.

"There's dozens of 'em." Vernon ran the topmost cloth through his fingers. "And they're all damaged."

"Not damaged," Seymour pointed out. "Someone made these holes."

Vernon took the cloth from Seymour and held it up to the light. He darted his fingers between each hole.

"And the holes make a shape," he said. "But why?"

Seymour smiled with sudden understanding.

"Hold it up at the window," he said.

With his brow furrowed, Vernon took the cloth to the window. He glanced outside, confirming that nobody was around, and then held it high.

"And?" he asked.

"I know what it is." Seymour held out his hands and they swapped positions.

Vernon stared at the cloth, rocking his head from side to side, and then shrugged.

"So what is it?"

"The black cloth represents the night sky. When light shines through the holes it'll form the shape of the constellations. In this case Orion."

Vernon frowned. "Like I said: what is it?"

"You've not looked at the night sky much, then?"

"Nope."

"Guessed as much." Seymour joined Vernon at the window and jabbed a finger against the cloth, tracing a pattern between each simulated star. "When you see Orion you know that winter's not far away."

"That's doesn't sound exciting." Vernon snorted. "If this is all he's showing, Sydney has nothing to worry about."

"But just to be sure . . ." Seymour reached down to his right boot and extracted a knife. "We'll give 'em something extra."

"That was a most interesting confession," Bishop Finnegan said, wiping an outbreak of sweat from his brow as he and Fergal left the chapel.

"I did limit myself to the ten most interesting things I've done," Fergal said, unperturbed.

"And I thank you for that." Finnegan frowned as Fergal directed him to head to the stables. "But what interests me the most is why you left out your most recent misdemeanor."

Fergal came to a halt. "What do you mean?"

Finnegan swung round to glare at him. "The fact that you find it hard to remember what your most recent failing has been concerns me more than the tale I heard in there. But let me help you. After the service, a troubled man by the name of Tucker Moorhead asked me a perturbing question."

"Oh?" Fergal murmured with due dread.

"He wanted to know when I was serving the whiskey. On further questioning, he revealed a worrying motivation for his attendance at tonight's service. Do I need to tell you what that motivation was?"

Fergal winced. When Woody had promised to entice people into the chapel, he'd expected him to offer a small cash inducement, but it would appear that he'd found a use for the barrel of whiskey he'd bought in Shinbone.

"No, but please don't hold that against anyone but me."

"I am not interested in excuses. The journey here was terrible. Sundown is appalling, the mission is crumbling, and now I find the only reason people attend services here is to get free liquor." Finnegan flashed a cold-eyed smile. "So I am in just the right frame of mind to appreciate the next item on your ill-advised evening of cultural pursuits, this display of authentic historical memorabilia."

He held out a hand, inviting Fergal to head into the stable first.

"I'm sure," Fergal said, smiling without much hope as he set off, "you'll find our display of religious relics to be most illuminating."

Once inside, Fergal pointed at the straight-backed duo of Woody and Randolph, who were standing behind a laid-out presentation of authentic religious exhibits.

"Before you continue with such boasts, I must warn you that in my travels I have seen many holy relics, all most welcome of course, but my attitude has become somewhat jaundiced over the years." Finnegan eyed the presentation with disdain. "In the last year alone I have seen Saint Peter's index finger, Saint Augustine's bottom rib, Saint Ignatius's big toe . . . Recently I even heard a tale of someone claiming to own something called the Treasure of Saint Woody, as if there were a saint called Woody."

Finnegan turned to Fergal and uttered a rare laugh. Fergal maintained his fixed grin and avoided looking at Woody, as he drew a blanket over his casket and then sidled away into the darkened recesses of the stable.

"Why can't there be a saint called Woody?" Fergal asked to keep Finnegan's attention on him and not spot that Woody was climbing over the stable wall.

"There can be a saint with such a name, but there isn't one."

"I have heard that said before, but how do you know that for sure?"

"Because the Church keeps good records and I believe I'd have noticed such a name." Finnegan considered Fergal's still unconvinced expression. "The process to become a saint is a lengthy one, often taking hundreds of years and the very learned and earnest consideration of many devoted men."

"And what do they consider?"

"Corroborated evidence of miracles performed by the individual is a good start."

"Interesting," Fergal murmured.

Then with Woody having dropped out of sight, he gestured, encouraging Finnegan to move on to consider the display of relics. The bishop maintained his stern expression, only changing it to one of irritation when his gaze fell on the first exhibit, a rather fresh-looking fish sitting beside a half-eaten loaf of bread.

"This is a holy relic?" he asked.

"Five thousand was a lot of people to feed," Fergal said, "and not everyone was that hungry. This is what was left over."

"No doubt." Finnegan walked past the bottle of water from Canaan, the rare one that didn't get turned into wine, and a clean cloth from Turin with the stain washed out. But he stopped at the next item, a stone cup. He peered at it. "And what, pray, is this?"

Randolph picked up the cup with due reverence and handed it to Finnegan. The soft piece of rock had been chiseled out, although the maker had been too enthusiastic in his work and had made a hole in the bottom.

"Be careful," Randolph said. "This is unique."

Finnegan turned the crudely made object over in his hands, frowning as he tried to discern what it was.

"I'm afraid you'll have to tell me what this is," he said finally.

"We searched for many years to find it," Randolph murmured, putting on an appropriately awed tone, "but we believe this to be not merely a cup, but a grail."

"A grail," Finnegan intoned. He stuck a finger through the hole. "A grail with a hole."

"And not just that. We believe this to be, in fact, the original and authentic holey—"

"Enough," Finnegan said, slamming the cup back down. "I can see that spelling was not a part of Father Brown's educational endeavors. I will leave you before you embarrass yourself further with this nonsense."

Finnegan moved off, leaving Fergal and Randolph to look at each other.

"Well, there's one thing I know for sure," Randolph said when Finnegan had left the stable. He held up a finger. "That's one failure."

Fergal presented two fingers with a sorry shake of the head.

"Two," he reported. "Apparently Woody bribed the people who came to the chapel with whiskey. Worse, Finnegan found out."

Randolph winced. "Then we'd better start praying that Thaddeus and Oliver both put on a performance of a lifetime, or we're doomed."

Fortified by their free whiskey, a snaking line of men was following Fergal and Randolph into the Mission Saloon.

Lost in the shadows beside the stable, Woody watched them. Tucker Moorhead would have revealed the truth about the whiskey bribe by now, so the evening would have gotten off to a bad start, or at least for Fergal and Randolph it would have . . .

A few minutes earlier, Vernon and Seymour had emerged from the El Hombre and stared in surprise at the men making an unexpected visit to the Mission Saloon.

Then Vernon had hurried back in, presumably to report to Sydney Grant, leaving Seymour to mosey across the road. He was whistling to himself and wandering aimlessly as he awaited further instructions. Ten yards from the stables, he stopped and looked up at the sky. He jerked around as if searching for something.

"You will not find anything of interest up there," Woody said, stepping into the light.

Seymour started, proving he didn't know Woody was there, and then lowered his gaze to him.

"I was looking for Orion, the gunslinger."

"I believe it is Orion, the hunter."

"Not anymore, it isn't," Seymour said with a chuckle. Then he moved to go but, with a deft sideways movement, Woody blocked his way.

"How will Sydney Grant react to the news that all these people are going into the Mission Saloon?"

Seymour smirked. "Badly."

"Is that because he wants Bishop Finnegan to abandon the mission, presumably so he can take it over?"

Seymour narrowed his eyes. "Why are you asking all these questions?"

"So I am right." Woody smiled with a brief upturn of the corners of his mouth. "But do not worry. I am just a showman who is interested in making money from the townsfolk of Sundown."

"With what you've got to offer, you'll never make a red cent."

"That statement is correct based on what you may have heard about Fergal's show, but you have not seen what I have to offer." Woody gestured to the stable door. "Follow me and you will be amazed."

Seymour didn't move, but when Woody raised his jacket to show that he wasn't armed, he followed. Silently they turned away from the straggling line of men who were still entering the saloon and went into the stable. There, Fergal and Randolph had packed away their authentic relics, but his blanket-clad casket was standing alone on the back of his wagon.

"What do you have to show me?" Seymour asked when they were standing before Woody's wagon.

"I will give you the opportunity to win the Treasure of Saint Woody."

"There's a saint called Woody?"

"There is."

Seymour narrowed his eyes. "And what is his treasure?"

"It has been rumored that it is the keys to heaven it-self."

Although Seymour sneered at this offer, the promise of a treasure made him join Woody in climbing onto the back of the wagon.

With a flourish, Woody removed the blanket to display the casket. It was closed and about six feet long, three feet high, and three feet wide. Bands of rusting iron covered each edge and the lid was rounded, but the jeweled circles on the lid that sparkled in the starlight coming down through the roofless stable drew Seymour's attention first. There were five and each contained twelve jewels.

Unbidden, Seymour fingered the jewels. Then he licked his lips, his interest now piqued.

"What do I do?" he asked.

Woody gestured at the circles, showing Seymour the ornate carvings of animals and people, and then nudged the first circle to a different position. With deft motions he moved the others, finishing with his finger pointing at a slot in the middle.

"You insert a coin. The circles turn and if they stop in an order that makes the carvings depict the life of Saint Woody, the casket will open."

Seymour scratched his head. "That sounds too hard to me."

He moved to go, but Woody thrust out an arm, stopping him, and nudged him back to the casket.

"Stick a coin in. Either you win or you do not. Is that simple enough for you?"

Seymour nodded. He rummaged in his pocket and located a dime, which he slipped into the slot. The coin landed inside with a tinkle and then rattled around the casket. Its motion made the jeweled circles turn.

With a grinding of gears, each circle revolved in the opposite direction to the circle beside it as, inside the casket, the dime rattled back and forth, taking a lengthy and complex route around the sides. Finally, the coin stopped rattling and, with a fateful clunk, the circles came to rest in the same position as they'd been in before.

Then a click sounded, followed by the casket lid springing up an inch.

"It opened," Seymour murmured.

"It did." Woody moved to stand at Seymour's shoulder. "You are now the proud owner of the Treasure of Saint Woody."

Seymour put a hand to the casket lid and slowly opened it. He held his breath while he levered the lid up to the vertical. At first the casket appeared to be empty, but when Seymour looked down into it, he saw the glittering twinkle of something shining inside.

The longer he looked, the more sparkling objects he saw.

"It really is treasure," he murmured. He moved in to scoop out a handful, but his hand closed on air.

He thrust his hand deeper into the casket and tried

again, but again he failed to hold on to any of the sparkling objects. Irritated now, he leaned right in and put a hand all the way to the bottom.

His fingers jarred against cold metal. This time the sparkling reduced, although among the spots of light, there was a dark mass that moved in time with his movements.

With a sudden change of perspective, he saw that the dark mass was, in fact, his own shadow, and that the sparkling objects were stars being reflected in the mirrorlike metal at the bottom of the casket.

He was about to confront Woody with this revelation when he saw a flaw on the bottom of the casket. He peered closer, seeing that it was writing. He moved from side to side to give himself enough light to see what was written there.

"Banging on the lid will not work," he read. This was such a strange thing to have been written there that he moved position again to see if he'd read this right, but then a second shadow loomed to his side.

"It will not," Woody said into his ear.

A dull thud sounded. The clatter of a large object hitting metal echoed through the stable.

Then a groan of pain sounded, cut off as the lid slammed shut.

Chapter Eight

Ma'am," Thaddeus exclaimed on bent knee, "you sure are a right pretty woman. If I were to look at a rose and then you, I wouldn't rightly know which were prettier."

Thaddeus jumped to his feet and swirled round to face the position he'd been kneeling in previously.

"Well, thank you kindly, young man," he intoned in the same loud voice.

Then he hurried over to the back of the stage and grabbed his sword.

"Get your dirty hands off her, Romeo," he boomed in a voice that was only slightly more assertive than the one he'd used for the previous tender scene, "or you'll buy yourself a one-way ticket to boot-hill."

He knelt. "You're wrong, Tybalt. My boots are staying on my feet while I kick your sorry hide out of town."

As Thaddeus jumped to his feet and mimed kicking himself, a subdued and bemused groan went up from

85

the packed audience, but at the bar Fergal leaned toward Randolph.

"What do you reckon to my words?" he asked.

"Got to hand it to you, Fergal," Randolph said, and then whistled through his teeth, "this play sure has some mighty fine dialogue."

"Not bad for a few hours' work." Fergal winced as Thaddeus managed to kick himself off the stage. "I just wish he could act."

Randolph nodded and, in his distracted state, he sipped the sarsaparilla Ophelia had poured for him. He winced, awaiting the cloying taste making an assault on his stomach, but to his surprise, it slipped down smoothly.

He decided this only showed that you could get used to anything, especially when he noticed that everyone in the audience, which in itself was far larger than he'd expected, was nursing a sarsaparilla while suffering the play.

The entire front row was staring up at Thaddeus in bemused shock while clutching their glasses to their chests, presumably in case one of Thaddeus' extravagant gestures with his sword swept it away. In the other rows, most of the men were spending more time staring into their glasses than looking at the stage. Bishop Finnegan was sitting in the back row, his own drink sitting by his chair untouched. His expression was one of stoic suffering.

"Well, I'll be a son of a gun," Thaddeus roared. "Parting sure is mighty sorrowful."

Randolph began to ask Fergal if he thought there was any hope that this artistic section of the night's show would change their fortunes when Finnegan made his plodding way over to them.

"I cannot deny that this man has enthusiasm," he said when he joined them at the bar, "but what is he doing with Shakespeare?"

"He is making it accessible to the common man," Fergal said.

"Then he has failed. This evening started badly, got worse, and now it has somehow worsened again."

Fergal offered a tentative smile. "But surely you're pleased to see that the people of Sundown are being catered to with all this art and culture?"

"Romeo, Romeo," Thaddeus yelled at the top of his voice, "where in tarnation are you?"

Finnegan's thin smile silently conveyed his answer. Then he returned to his seat, leaving Fergal and Randolph to watch Thaddeus emote.

Presently, with one last bellowed declaration about a happy gun, Thaddeus thankfully died, twice. After which he jumped to his feet to take the applause from the audience, although the only response he got was a stampede to the bar to order more sarsaparillas.

Fergal leaned toward Randolph and showed him three fingers.

"I reckon that's three failures," he said.

"It is," Randolph said. "Which mean all our hopes lie with Oliver."

Fergal nodded, but then found himself buffeted away from the bar by the press of people.

"At least he'll have a proper audience, and they're all enjoying their healthy drinks, so there must be some hope."

"But why?" Randolph swirled a finger in the foam and then shrugged. "Nobody liked the sarsaparillas before."

"Perhaps Woody's offered them whiskey if they came." Fergal looked around. "And for that matter, where is Woody? I have something to say to him about how he filled the chapel."

Randolph smiled. "I reckon he knows that too. That's why he's gone to ground."

Fergal nodded, then returned to watching Ophelia serve sarsaparillas. But despite their concerns, nobody left and within five minutes, nearly everyone had returned to their chairs.

Contented chatter filled the saloon. The only zone of disquiet was Thaddeus, who had ordered a double sarsaparilla and was gulping it down with steady determination, while glaring at the audience.

Fergal picked out Finnegan, who was also considering the people milling about, but he was doing so without his usual scowl. Before Fergal could go over to him to reinforce one of the few successful aspects of the evening, he saw that Oliver was bustling around on the stage.

Fergal hitched his jacket and turned from the bar.

"Right," he said to himself. "Phenomenon, phenomenon, phenomenon."

Randolph patted him on the shoulder and murmured a few words of encouragement. Then Fergal headed over to Oliver.

The scientist had already set up a lectern, an upturned barrel, and behind it, he'd piled up the heap of black cloth. For ease of handling, each piece lay as alternative squares and diamonds. Beside the lectern stood a square frame, which Oliver had set upright to face the audience. Behind the frame an unlit oil lamp stood on a table.

Fergal fingered the topmost cloth, shaking his head in bemusement as he wondered what Oliver would do with it, and then stood behind the lectern. Only a few seats were unoccupied, with the stragglers having yet to be served. He judged this the right moment to begin and so he gestured to the crowd with his palms facing downward until the contented chatter reduced to a level that let him speak.

"Gentlemen," he announced, "the Mission Saloon is renowned for its educational, artistic, and cultural endeavors."

"Since when?" Tucker Moorhead shouted from the front row.

Fergal ignored him and continued. "Tonight, for your

edification and delight, I have the great pleasure of introducing the world's foremost expert on astronomy, who will talk to us about the greatest visual display we will ever witness, which will happen tomorrow. So without further ado, I present to you Oliver Rhinehart and his lecture on stellar phenom . . . stellar phenomen . . . his lecture on starry stuff."

To a smattering of applause, along with calls to keep the sarsaparillas coming, Oliver stepped up to the lectern with his head bowed and a bundle of papers thrust under an arm. With a nervous glance at the audience, he ruffled his notes and banged them on the lectern. He coughed twice, placed his notes before him, and began reading.

"Good evening, gentlemen," he said, his voice low. "Welcome to tonight's lecture."

"Speak up," Tucker said.

Oliver coughed, then raised his notes again and lowered his voice.

"My lecture tonight is on the causes, nature, and processes that deliver the marvelous phenomenon of the solar eclipse. I will—"

"Speak up."

Oliver looked up. "I'm speaking as loudly as I can."

"But I still can't hear you." Tucker looked around, receiving a cascade of nods from the second row.

"Perhaps it's the acoustic limitations in this saloon. This isn't a lecture hall and everyone is making so much noise. Can you hear me at the back?" Oliver looked at

Finnegan, who was staring at his hands. When long moments had passed and the bishop continued to look down, he waved his notes above his head. "I said, can you hear me at the back, Your Excellency?"

"Pardon?" Finnegan said, looking up.

Oliver took a deep breath. "Can you hear my lecture?"

"What lecture?"

Oliver winced, and then looked to Randolph for help, but Thaddeus brightened and took the duty upon himself. In the booming voice he'd used for his romantic scenes, he demanded quiet and then shooed away the customers who were still clamoring for sarsaparillas.

When all had settled down in their seats and quiet had descended, Oliver smiled.

"Can you hear me now?" he asked.

"Hear what?" Tucker said.

"Hear . . ." Oliver saw that Tucker was smiling, so he returned to reading his notes. "Tonight, I will cover all aspects of planetary orbits, the eclipses that have occurred throughout history, and the scientific advances that we have made from observation of those eclipses before ending with an introduction to the night sky. But first, to understand the—"

"Speak up."

Oliver glared at Tucker. "Would you please stop interrupting me."

"Then speak up. You start speaking loud enough, and then you mumble."

"I'm sorry." Oliver coughed and continued in the same low voice. "To understand the events that will take place, we must first consider the history of the universe."

"Speak . . ."

Oliver looked up. "Is that loud enough or not?"

"Did you say that you're about to lecture us on the history of the universe?"

"I am."

"Then that's loud enough." Tucker shuffled down in his chair and lowered his hat over his face.

Oliver picked up his notes and continued reading.

"The ancient Greeks conceptualized the universe in a geocentric manner, that is, placing the earth at the center of the universe. This view held firm for many centuries."

From the front row, a rasping snore escaped Tucker's lips.

"Explain to me why I employed you," Sydney Grant muttered.

"To keep trouble away from El Hombre," Hank Kelly said.

"And you've certainly succeeded," Sydney said, gesturing at the deserted saloon. "It's just a pity that you did it by driving away all my customers."

"That's not our fault."

"Did you not bring Oliver Rhinehart to town?"

"We did, and I told you he'd improve takings, but

you turned him down." When his defiance made Sydney flare his eyes, Hank spread his hands. "But I'm as surprised as you are that everyone has deserted the El Hombre and gone to the Mission Saloon to hear a lecture on astronomy."

"I don't concern myself with the details. I just know that all I can hear over here is silence, and all I can hear over there is the sound of people enjoying themselves." Sydney shook a fist. "And I have no idea how he's doing it."

"It's because of me," a new voice intoned from the doorway.

Sydney swirled round to find that Woody had arrived in the saloon. He stood a few paces in from the door, his stove hat placed at a jaunty angle, his feet set wide apart.

"That's a mighty brave thing for an unarmed man to claim."

"It is not, when I have ensured that tonight will be a disaster for the Mission Saloon." He pointed at Hank and Vernon. "You employ men who are proficient with guns and fists, but I prefer a more subtle approach. Soon, just when it looks as if the night will end in triumph, Bishop Finnegan will discover what I have done."

Sydney smiled. "Which is?"

"Unbeknown to Ophelia Green, the customers she has unexpectedly attracted are not there to listen to Oliver." Woody paced across the saloon room, placing each foot to the floor with steady care. "They are there because her healthy drinks have an interesting new formula—sarsaparillas with rye extract!"

Sydney chuckled. "A temperance saloon serving liquor won't be popular with Bishop Finnegan. But why did you do it?"

"Because your associate Seymour told me some interesting things about your desire for Bishop Finnegan to close the mission."

Sydney slammed a fist on the bar in irritation.

"That Seymour talks too much." He shot a glance at Hank. "Make sure he learns to keep his mouth shut."

"I will," Hank said, then glanced around. "Although I haven't seen him for a while. I'll—"

"Be quiet. I'm interested in what Woody has to say, not in your prattle."

"And so you should be," Woody said, as he stopped before the bar. "I am here to ensure that all your dreams come true."

"I thought you were with Fergal and Randolph?"

"I was, but they have limited ambition, so I have decided to end our partnership. As I feel that you and I are more in tune with, shall we say, what is required to succeed, our partnership has just begun."

Sydney frowned. "What are you implying?"

"I never imply. I only state. Two years ago three nuns were killed here. Father Brown stayed on, but then he was killed. I believe you know more about those events than most."

Sydney narrowed his eyes and cast a quick warning glance at Hank and Vernon.

"So," he said guardedly, "are you aiming to make me pay to keep that information secret?"

Woody spread his hands in a benevolent gesture, although his expression remained stern.

"Nothing of the sort. In fact, I am aiming to help you." Woody leaned over the bar and raised his hat. "I might even bring you the keys to heaven itself."

"The presence of an elliptical orbit," Oliver murmured, hidden behind his notes, "leads to variations in the apparent diameter of the secondary object from its mean of thirty arc minutes."

Oliver lowered his notes and offered a tentative smile.

Randolph and Fergal sat at the bar in a hunched and muttering huddle. Ophelia had just returned from checking on Maria and was making a valiant attempt to keep up with the demand for sarsaparillas. In the front row, Tucker delivered another rasping snore while elsewhere all attention was on the poker games that were in progress. The only person listening to Oliver was Bishop Finnegan, and he was sitting with folded arms while glowering at him.

Oliver hid behind his notes again. "But the consequences of such aberrations are exasperated by the fact that . . ."

Oliver turned over a page.

Finnegan stretched and then leaned down to pick up his sarsaparilla from the floor. He moved it toward his lips, but then thought better of it and raised a hand.

Oliver pointed at him. "You have a question, Your Excellency?"

"I do." Finnegan covered a yawn. "I've had a long, tiring, and pointless day. How much longer will this take?"

Oliver glanced at his notes. "I am nearly halfway through my notes, although I have set aside time for questions before my presentation of the night sky. But if anyone wants to ask anything now, please do so."

"And you'll only answer questions about stellar phenomenon?"

"Yes."

"In that case, no."

"What happened?" Tucker said, his arms waving and his boots slamming to the floor as he suddenly woke up.

Everyone around him chuckled.

"You was asleep," Finnegan said. "Now you're awake. That's what happened."

Tucker yawned and stretched, throwing out his arms to their utmost.

"How much longer will this take?"

"He's nearly halfway through, but he's put aside time for questions before his presentation of the night sky, although he will take questions now."

"Then I have a question now." Tucker took a deep

breath and glared up at Oliver. "What in tarnation are you blathering on about?"

Oliver gulped and then glanced at his notes. "I am describing the dynamics of orbital eccentricity and its impact on the incidence of eclipses."

Tucker rubbed his brow. "Obliged. Carry on."

Oliver ruffled his notes and cleared his throat.

"The primary object also has an apparent diameter of thirty arc minutes, so—"

"Are you still talking about ancient times?" Tucker said.

"Sorry?"

"When I fell asleep, you was talking about the history of the universe and them there Greeks. Are you now talking about the Ark?"

"No, I am not." Oliver lowered his head, sighed, placed his notes on the lectern, and then mimed a ball shape. "I am talking about the apparent diameter of a spherical object when viewed from the earth."

"What spherical object?"

"The moon!" Oliver shouted, stamping his foot for emphasis. He looked at the blank and bored faces of his audience. "Perhaps . . . perhaps I should demonstrate with something round."

"Such as?" Tucker asked, sounding interested for the first time.

"Your head," Oliver snapped.

Everyone chuckled. The poker players lowered their

cards. Several people stopped drinking their sarsaparillas to look up.

Tucker rolled to his feet. "Sounds a good idea. Demonstrate your Ark thing with my head."

Oliver nodded. "With pleasure. I will need two people."

Finnegan stood from where he'd been brooding in the back row.

"I'll volunteer in the hope it'll get this over with quickly," he said.

"Thank you. I also need someone with a bigger head than Tucker's."

"I reckon," Thaddeus boomed, standing and giving his moustache a tweak, "I have the biggest head around here."

Predictable comments greeted this declaration, while Oliver directed Tucker to stand before the stage and Thaddeus to stand by the wall. He positioned Finnegan in a direct line to them.

"Now, Your Excellency, I'll ask you to pretend that Thaddeus' head is the sun and that Tucker's head is the moon. From your position, you'll see that Tucker's head obscures Thaddeus' head."

"That's obvious," Finnegan said, squinting with an eye closed at Tucker. "All you're saying is that Tucker has the smaller head, but he's nearer, so he obscures Thaddeus' larger head, which is farther away."

Oliver nodded. "You are quite right."

Finnegan scratched his brow. "And that means that

although the moon is smaller than the sun, because it's nearer to us, it obscures the larger sun and creates an eclipse."

A round of applause greeted his explanation.

"It does not," Thaddeus proclaimed. "Juliet is the sun and she kills the envious moon."

"In this case she does not," Oliver said. "As I've been saying for the last half hour, the apparent diameter of an object at a distance of . . ." Oliver glanced at his notes, rubbed his chin, and then placed his papers on the lectern. "Now with that matter clarified, I will move on to explain why planetary objects follow elliptical orbits. And to explain that, I need to explain gravity."

"Shall we go back to our seats?" Tucker asked.

Oliver nodded, and then raised a hand, halting everyone.

"No, I think I can explain this in a more visual manner too."

Oliver looked around the room. His gaze fell on the food Ophelia had laid out to cook up after the lecture. He headed to the table as everyone watched and murmured with sudden interest. He returned with a basket containing several eggs.

"And what are you going to do with that basket?" Tucker asked.

"You'll find out." Oliver smiled. "Provided you're prepared to help me with another demonstration."

Tucker grinned. "Sure would like to help."

"Good. For my demonstration of how gravity works, I will again use Tucker's head." Oliver reached into the basket and then held his hand aloft. "And this raw egg."

Everyone leaned forward.

Chapter Nine

It's actually working," Randolph said, leaning toward Fergal during a brief break in the lecture.

"The cost of all those eggs Oliver dropped on Tucker's head will be a bit high," Fergal said. Then he smiled and rubbed his hands. "But it looks as if it was worth it."

Both men looked at Bishop Finnegan, who was now smiling. The last half hour had been raucous, after Oliver had finally become entertaining, but even the most mean-spirited of men couldn't deny that the atmosphere had been good-natured.

"My favorite part," Randolph said, "was when Oliver demonstrated how meteors burn up by setting fire to Tucker's pants."

Ophelia broke off from serving to favor them with a mischievous smile.

"Many people have taken the view," she said, "that any night could be enlivened by setting fire to Tucker's pants."

Fergal and Randolph both laughed before the milling people around the bar took her out of view. Then, with Oliver signifying that he was ready to finish off his lecture with his promised stunning finale, Fergal hurried to the stage.

Fergal picked out Finnegan, noted that he was still smiling, and raised his arms in a call for quiet. Unlike the previous time, silence descended within seconds, and the crowd hurried back to their chairs, clutching their sarsaparillas, eager to see what Oliver would do next.

Even the somewhat sticky and singed-around-the-edges Tucker was smiling.

Fergal signaled to Randolph, who dimmed the oil lamps around the saloon until the only light entering the room came from the window. Then, while Fergal hurried over to shutter the window, extinguishing even that gleam, Oliver lit the oil lamp behind the frame on the table, creating a homely glow at the back of the saloon.

Subdued chatter filled the room. Chairs scuffed as people craned their necks to see what he was doing. Then demands to settle down rippled around the room.

Oliver dimmed the lamplight until he had the level he required. Then he took the topmost square and held it in his left hand. He stood beside the lectern and faced the audience.

Total silence returned in seconds.

"To close tonight's astronomy lecture," he announced in a firm voice that filled the room, with all signs of his earlier tentative delivery gone, "I will present to you the wonder that is the night sky. I will introduce a series of illustrations of the shapes that stars make. We call these shapes constellations. Some constellations may be familiar and some not, but with my illustrated guide, the night sky will never be the same again."

With a whip of his hand, Oliver placed the cloth over the frame and stood back.

"This first illustration is of that most familiar of winter constellations, Orion."

The audience stared at the cloth and the small points of light the oil lamp created through the holes. The flame's flickering light even made the simulated stars twinkle as they shone across the saloon.

The front row glanced at each other. The starlight dappled their bemused faces as the second row replicated their movement, which then rippled back through the rows. A nervous titter emerged from a man in the third row, followed by a fit of coughing.

Oliver folded his arms. "Before I talk about Orion, I should say that I'm happy to take questions at any stage."

The audience shuffled in their seats until Tucker raised a hand. Oliver pointed at him.

"I'd guessed you might have a question, Mr. Moorhead," he said, smiling. "What is it?"

"What did Orion do?" Tucker asked.

"He was a hunter."

"Was he any good at it?"

"He was. In fact, killing too many animals was his downfall, as he slew all before him with his mighty sword."

Titters rippled around the audience.

"And was he fearsome?"

"As a hunter he made many enemies. But he was fearless and so that didn't worry him."

"That wasn't what I meant." Tucker took a deep breath. "I meant would he win a showdown against a gunslinger like, say, Tex Porter?"

Oliver shrugged. "A man with a sword would never win a showdown against a man with a gun."

Tucker smirked. "I reckon you're right. So I guess that's why he's shooting off such a huge gun."

An explosion of laughter echoed through the saloon. Oliver stepped off the stage and looked at his cloth as the laughter continued. His eyes narrowed, forcing his mind to register the unexpected arrangement of holes. He gulped.

With a lunge, he ripped away the cloth and threw it to the side. He picked up the next cloth.

"Moving on to the next display," he murmured, a shaking voice replacing his short-lived assured delivery. "This cloth depicts the mythical horse Pegasus. Now,

this constellation is harder to make out than Orion was."
Oliver placed the cloth over the frame and smoothed
it. "But I'm sure with my help you will be able to
see—"

"That's a horse all right," Tucker said. "No trouble
making that out."

"You have a good imagination. Most people can't
see a horse in this arrangement of stars."

"It's clear to me." Tucker rubbed his chin and rocked
his head to the side. "Would Pegasus be Orion's horse
by any chance?"

"No."

"Surprising. He sure looks to be a mighty fast steed.
He's galloping faster than that train."

Oliver backed over the edge of the stage and stared
at the cloth. He shook his head and edged back another
pace to stand before the first row. The light twinkled
through the holes in the cloth and presented a far better
depiction of a horse than the night sky had ever managed.

Then his eyes widened.

"I'm sorry," he said, slapping his forehead. "There
seems to have been some mistake here. I'm sure the ancient Greeks didn't know about trains."

"Don't worry," Tucker said. "These illustrations are
most educational. Carry on."

Oliver shuffled to his cloth pile. With a bemused shake

of the head he removed Pegasus and fixed the next cloth over the frame.

"Now this is perhaps the most familiar of all constellations." Oliver took a deep breath as he pushed it into position. "It is of the Great Bear."

"What's the great bear doing?" Tucker asked.

Oliver stood back and then winced. "The popular depiction is of the bear on all fours, but here he appears to be . . ." He held his head to the side. "I wouldn't like to say."

"That great bear seems to have produced a great pile of—"

"Please accept that not all of the holes are in the exact same positions as you'll find in the night sky." Oliver glanced to the bar but received a bewildered shrug from Fergal. "I believe there has been some augmentation to aid in the process of understanding."

"Are those stars supposed to represent steam rising?" Tucker asked.

Oliver ignored him. He ripped down the cloth and, with a loud and worried gulp, he hung the next one on the frame.

A wave of silence spread through the saloon. Jaws dropped.

The only member of the audience not to stare with his mouth wide open was Finnegan, who was so shocked that he raised his as yet untouched sarsaparilla to his mouth. With the offending picture distracting him, he took a sip, and then licked his lips, appearing pleased.

Then he sniffed the foam. Confusion wrinkled his brow before his eyes flared. He tore his gaze away from the drink to pick out Ophelia with a glare that was so piercing she couldn't help but look at him.

As the audience started to chuckle, the sound growing as they got over their surprise, Randolph and Fergal turned to each other at the bar. Both men held up four fingers. Then Fergal grabbed the nearest sarsaparilla and downed it. Curiously the taste made him nod approvingly.

"The next illustration is of Virgo, the sweetest maiden of them all," Oliver said, his voice shaking, as he edged back for a pace to see what was causing the consternation. Then he clamped a hand over his face and peered at the cloth through his splayed fingers. "Although you wouldn't think so from this illustration."

"The mission closes tomorrow, Ophelia," Bishop Finnegan said when she joined him in the chapel. "I will not waste another cent of the Church's money on this . . . this place."

"But you must have seen the progress Father Brown made here," Ophelia murmured, without much hope.

"No doubt his work was rewarding, but I am saddened to say that I have visited outposts in the jungles of South America that are more promising than Sundown."

"It was hard to achieve anything, which made the work even more important, and you saw that at least the town does fulfill some of your requirements."

"Admittedly the town is less dangerous than I feared it would be, but as for the rest . . ." Finnegan held up a hand and then counted off his concerns on his fingers. "The chapel was full, but only because of an offer of free liquor. What passes for culture is a huckster showing dubious relics he no doubt made himself. Art involves getting an earache from a buffoon's cowboy version of Shakespeare. As for the educational endeavors, I fear I will never again look at the night sky with wonder. But worst of all, you were serving liquor in the mission."

"I . . . I didn't know that. And we are helping some." Ophelia leaned forward and tried the only plea she was sure would not fall on deaf ears. "Maria gives solace to many who are in need."

"I have seen no sign of her apparent miracles helping anyone. I have seen only signs of you helping her." He softened his tone. "But I won't let her suffer. When I leave, I will take her with me, and I will ensure she gets the best possible care for whatever time she has left. But this place can return to the ground."

"Is there anything I can say or do to change your mind?"

Finnegan laid a friendly hand on Ophelia's shoulder and offered an understanding tone.

"It would need a miracle."

"Woody has betrayed us," Fergal said. "He's joined Sydney Grant."

Randolph rubbed his hands. "Good. I've had enough of that creepy man."

Fergal considered the deserted Mission Saloon. After Bishop Finnegan's discovery that the sarsaparillas had been spiked, everyone returned to the El Hombre, from where the sounds of revelry were growing.

Ophelia and Finnegan had gone to the chapel, presumably not to tell her good news, while Thaddeus and Oliver had cleared away the mess, and then left to bed down in the stable.

"Creepy or not," Fergal said, with a determined shake of a bony fist, "I will make him pay for turning on us and destroying Ophelia's chances of keeping the mission open."

"Glad to see he's not destroyed your spirit." Randolph waited until Fergal nodded, and then leaned toward him and lowered his voice. "But just remember there's a line here you can't cross. An ill woman's future is at stake, and no matter how much we want revenge against Woody, you mustn't do anything that would offend Ophelia."

Randolph looked at Fergal through narrowed eyes to

reinforce his demand. Then with a slap on his shoulder, Randolph headed off to their wagon, leaving him to ruminate.

Fergal followed Randolph to the door, where he stopped and watched him disappear into the stable. Then he turned to the El Hombre.

Customers were visible through the broken window, their brisk movements and bursts of raucous singing evidence that they were enjoying themselves. He couldn't see Woody, but he vowed that the next time he saw him, he would already have a plan in operation to defeat him.

Then he headed back into the Mission saloon. He walked across the empty room and through the back store to come out facing the chapel. A light inside showed that Ophelia and Finnegan were still there talking.

Backing onto the store was a leaning timber structure that Ophelia had erected to house herself and Maria.

Fergal took a deep breath and then lowered his head to slip inside. An oil lamp beside Maria's bed was turned down low, but it was still bright enough to illuminate her sleeping face.

Fergal looked at her, wondering if there was something obvious he'd missed when he'd given her his tonic yesterday, but no ideas would come.

"How are you?" he asked.

He waited for an answer, but when one didn't come, he rocked from foot to foot, feeling awkward. Then he regained his composure by withdrawing a bottle from his pocket.

"I've made this new tonic," he said, going over to the bed. "It's stronger than the last one. I hope it'll work this time."

He waggled the bottle. The amber liquid caught the light and the strong brew cast bright flashes across her face, making her appear animated and heartening him.

"And while you drink this down, I'll discuss something with you." Fergal uncorked the bottle and moved it toward her lips. "To save the mission, I may have to cross the line."

Sydney Grant whistled as he locked the evening's takings in the safe.

With his customers spending half the evening in the Mission Saloon, he hadn't made as much tonight as he normally made, but Woody's welcome and effective help had improved his spirits.

He turned, aiming to retire for the night, but found Woody standing behind him in the doorway behind the bar.

"Were you spying on me?" Sydney murmured, when his heart had stopped thudding.

Woody dismissed the matter of his quiet arrival with a wave.

"I have no need to do that." He considered the safe. "Why not keep your money in the bank?"

"Bandits could ride in and steal it. I prefer to make my own arrangements."

"Then I should point out that Hank and Vernon were showing an unnatural level of interest in your safe earlier."

"Obliged for the information," Sydney said, guardedly.

"I thought it best to mention, especially with all the money we will be making." Woody returned to the saloon room and stood before the bar. "So now that everyone has retired, this is a good time to discuss our future."

"Perhaps tomorrow," Sydney said, as he leaned on the bar facing him, "after we know for sure what's happening to the mission."

"I believe that after tonight's debacle, Bishop Finnegan has already decided to abandon the mission." Woody waited while Sydney shook a fist in triumph. "And so, after that . . . ?"

Sydney poured himself a celebratory whiskey.

"To be honest, I hadn't thought too much about what I'd do after I have the mission. All I know for sure is I'll make the best buildings into a home and use the chapel for another saloon."

"And that is the limit of your ambition, is it?"

Sydney downed his whiskey in a single gulp.

"You said you can offer me more, even the keys to heaven itself, so what magnificent level of ambition do you have?"

The sarcasm didn't change Woody's impassive expression.

"After Oliver's version of the night sky, Ophelia will not allow him to perform again, so tomorrow we can make money from the eclipse." Woody raised a hand as Sydney started to cast doubt on the chances of that working. Then he drew his attention to the casket standing by the far wall. "That will give us the funds to make a fortune from the Treasure of Saint Woody."

"When did you bring that in here?" Sydney waited for an answer that didn't come, and then walked around the bar and over to the casket. "And why do you think this box will make a fortune?"

"This *casket* is just the start. I will build another ten just like it, and maybe one day even a hundred."

"Why bother? This one doesn't look interesting."

"You just need to appreciate its subtleties." Woody gestured along the wall. "Soon this wall will be filled with caskets like this one, each having a different secret combination, each requiring the insertion of a different value of coin, and each offering a different reward to the winner."

Sydney looked down at the casket. "And what is the reward for getting into this one?"

"As I said earlier, some say it is the keys to heaven itself, but that is the offer to the customer. Only we know the truth. That money goes in, but only we collect."

Sydney shrugged. "It's a vision, I guess, but it's not one I share. Confirmation that Bishop Finnegan has abandoned the mission will be enough to satisfy me."

Sydney moved to go upstairs, but Woody blocked his way with a quick sideways movement.

"If that is your wish, so be it, but grant me one attempt to change your mind. Try the casket and see if you enjoy what it has to offer. Who knows, you may even win those keys to heaven."

Sydney looked at the casket. "I guess I owe you that, but I don't reckon I'll ever want to try it again."

"I am sure you will not," Woody said.

Fergal stood in the doorway to the Mission Saloon looking up at the night sky, trying to imagine that Taurus, the rampaging longhorn, was really tossing a cowpuncher over its head as in Oliver's amended depiction.

He couldn't see it.

Randolph had retired some time ago, but Fergal didn't think he could sleep.

The stronger tonic he'd given Maria hadn't worked. She hadn't shown even a glimmer of movement to suggest the brew had affected her, and Fergal didn't think he could make the tonic any stronger.

He had always had a theory that his tonic worked on people who had a good heart, explaining why it usually gave its buyers a bellyache, but Maria's failure to respond had shaken that belief.

Fergal had just turned his attention to seeking out the Gemini twins' gun-toting showdown when he found he wasn't the only one with something on his mind. Thaddeus arrived, mooching along.

"I am troubled," Thaddeus announced, with a theatrically clenched fist held to his heart.

He joined Fergal and both men looked up at the star-filled sky in silent contemplation.

"What's wrong?" Fergal said finally.

"Tonight's play did not get the reception I had hoped for. And I know why." Thaddeus produced a sheaf of papers from behind his back and waved them at him. "The play wasn't Shakespeare."

"Too right." Fergal slammed a finger on the nearest page, picking out one of his amendments. "This time it was good."

"And to cater to the basest of emotions," Thaddeus whined, slapping a fist to his forehead in a show of being miserable, "I sold my soul."

"Giving people what they want isn't selling your soul."

"I wasn't referring to my audience. I meant me." Thaddeus glanced around, confirming nobody else was close. "I agreed to let you rewrite Shakespeare for dishonorable reasons. I wanted to perform just once before a large audience. I thought the changes would make them adore me, but they did not."

Fergal winced. "We both made that mistake. But people do mad things sometimes. Isn't that what happens in your play?"

"That and swordplay." Thaddeus rolled up the papers and held them aloft, his morose state forgotten. "My adoring public love to see me lunge across the stage."

Thaddeus danced and thrust his papers forward, as if they were a sword that he was sticking into an imaginary foe.

Fergal sighed. "Do you know how to use a sword or are you just acting?"

Thaddeus fingered his moustache. "And that is the beauty of theater when it's performed by a master of the craft. I've made you wonder whether I have the skill or whether I'm acting."

"I know exactly what you are," Fergal said as Thaddeus leaped back and forth, swishing his papers with each leap.

"But tonight was a disaster. So from now on I will use my sword more often, and no matter what you say, I will not take any more Shakespeare out."

Thaddeus gestured with the papers at Fergal, as if he were holding him at sword point, threatening to run him through if he didn't agree, but an idea had just come to Fergal.

"I'm not saying you should. I reckon you could even put some Shakespeare back in." Fergal moved round to stand beside Thaddeus and, with a hand on his shoulder, he lowered the papers. "It shouldn't offend too many people, because the way I see it, it's not what you say or do. It's the drama of the situation."

"I do not agree. Clear speaking is what people want." Thaddeus tucked a thumb behind a lapel and beamed while holding a hand aloft. "But I can see that the theater bug has bitten you."

"Maybe it has. And to increase the drama, you need a dramatic backdrop to your clear speaking." Fergal thrust a hand aloft, matching Thaddeus' actor posture. "And I ask you, what is more dramatic than an eclipse?"

"Aside from my acting?"

"Aside from that."

"Then nothing."

Fergal shuffled nearer to Thaddeus. "Exactly. According to Oliver, the sky will blacken, a chill wind will freeze our bones, and night animals will emerge, blinking and eager, and day ones will scurry into hiding."

"I'm impressed. You look at life in a creative manner when you're not writing silly dialogue."

"Yup. And I've been thinking that if you were to stage your play again tomorrow, but this time during the eclipse, the darkening sky will intensify the drama. And if you were to time your most dramatic lines for the precise moment the sky blackens, the effect will be tremendous."

"I can see that." Thaddeus leaped to the side to provide an imaginary triumphant sword thrust, and then placed a hand to his heart. "I can't believe there'd be a more wondrous sight."

"Even better if you did it outside." Fergal directed him to look down the road. "Say, in the road, outside the

El Hombre. Tights-clad, on bent knee, sword in hand, with the eclipsed sun high above you. It'll create an image that'll live in the townsfolk's memories for the rest of their lives."

Thaddeus fingered his moustache. "It will be my finest moment."

They basked in the glory of this triumphant vision for a full minute before Fergal leaned toward him and lowered his voice.

"And now that I've helped you," he said, "maybe you could help me. I'd like some advice on stagecraft."

"Nobody knows more about enchanting an audience than I," Thaddeus said, poised in heroic stance. "What kind of majesty of the stage were you interested in?"

"Staging a miracle," Fergal said.

Chapter Ten

An hour after sunup on the morning of the eclipse, Randolph woke to hammering and shouting. He went to the stable door and looked outside.

A line of workers was heading by, but the main activity was out of his view on the edge of town. As Fergal had left town late last night and hadn't returned yet, Randolph had nothing to occupy his mind and so he headed to the Mission Saloon.

Ophelia was sweeping out the room. She broke off to give him a frown that acknowledged the troubles they'd had last night.

"Sarsaparilla?" she asked.

"Maybe later," Randolph said. "I just came to see how Maria is."

"There's been no change." She extracted a familiarly shaped bottle from her pocket. "So tell Fergal to stay away from her. I won't let him use any more of his snake oil remedies on her."

Randolph winced. "You mean you let him try again?"

"No," she snapped. "That's the problem. He must have sneaked in here last night and . . . and . . ."

Seeing her being lost for words, Randolph raised a hand.

"I'm sorry, but I'm sure Fergal meant well."

She slapped her broom to the floor with a clatter, glared at him for a moment, but then offered a tense smile.

"I guess. I'm not angry with you. But he shouldn't have fed her his tonic without my permission, whether he meant well or not."

With her anger having abated, Randolph gnawed at his lip, searching for something else to say.

"And what will you do now?"

"Without the Church's help, I can't support myself on the occasional meal and even more occasional sarsaparilla, so I'll leave. Where to, I don't know." She looked around the saloon and sighed. "This place isn't much, but it's been my home for the last three years. I'll miss it."

"And Maria?"

"Bishop Finnegan says he'll find some nuns who will care for her. I'll miss her too."

Randolph heard the catch in her throat, so he didn't press for more details. After they'd stood in silence for a while, she returned to her sweeping and he left the saloon.

A steady stream of people were still making their way past, and this time Randolph joined them. He soon saw that a group of men was erecting an enclosure on the edge of town.

Ten yards from the fence, he stopped, and with his arms folded, he watched the workers bustle as they erected awnings and seating around a central clear space.

He couldn't see Sydney Grant among the crowd, although he could see Woody directing the operations. After several minutes, Woody happened to see him. He provided a few orders and then wended his way through the workers and over the fence to join him.

"Are you thinking of coming here as a paying customer, or to cause trouble?" he asked, leaning back against the fence.

"It depends on what you're showing."

Woody pointed upward. "The eclipse, of course. After Oliver's stunning success last night, although not in Bishop Finnegan's eyes, everyone is keen to see him present the eclipse, with the added benefit of enjoying sarsaparillas with rye extract—without the sarsaparilla."

Randolph looked around. "And where's Sydney Grant?"

"He went away. I am now the owner of El Hombre."

Randolph stared at Woody, wondering if this was true, but when Woody stared back impassively, he shrugged and moved over to stand beside him.

"So how much will this show cost to see?"

"Ten dollars, as the sign says." Woody picked up a freshly painted sign from the ground and held it up for inspection.

"Professor Oliver Rhinehart's Amazing Display of Stellar Phenomenon!" Randolph said, reading the rest of the sign. *"Be astounded by a show that will light up your life!"*

"A fair price for the greatest show ever."

Randolph sighed. "With the little we've made this week, ten dollars is a lot of money."

Woody gestured. "Look around. These seats say that I believe I am right. This eclipse is the greatest money-making idea ever to come to Sundown. You were wrong to waste your time on Maria and Ophelia's problems when you could have been part of this."

Randolph firmed his jaw, refusing to let Woody rile him, but Woody's raised voice made two passersby stop to see what the debate was about.

"It still doesn't seem worth it to me," Randolph said, loud enough to ensure they could hear him.

"It is." Woody gestured at the people. "Ignore him. He is just bitter."

The argument made three more people stop to watch, so with his audience growing, Randolph set his hands on his hips and moved to the side so that he could address everyone.

"I just don't want to waste my money without assurance that this show will be worth it."

"Anyone who saw Oliver's show last night knows that when he says something is amazing, it is." Woody nodded to the gathering, receiving a cheer. Heartened, he raised his voice. "But I will offer this assurance: if this is not the greatest show ever, you will get your money back."

The gathering grunted with approval, but Randolph snorted.

"If I was so sure, I'd make the offer that this will be the greatest show ever—or ten times your money back."

Woody jutted his chin. "Then I will."

Randolph staggered backward for a pace, letting his mouth fall open to register surprise.

"You must be mighty sure. I . . . I offer my most sincere apology for ever doubting you."

Woody narrowed his eyes as he considered Randolph's overstated performance, the likes of which he'd seen several times before when he'd been cured by Fergal's tonic.

"Apology accepted," he said cautiously. "And will you be here this afternoon?"

"Sure will." Randolph coughed to suppress a grin. "I wouldn't miss this for anything."

"You're late," Randolph said, when Fergal returned in early afternoon.

"I had a lot to do," Fergal said, jumping down from his wagon. "Is everything going according to plan?"

"Sure. Woody is putting on a show. Bishop Finnegan

is praying in the chapel. Thaddeus is shining up his sword. Ophelia wants to wring your neck. And you?"

Fergal spread his thin arms to display his bright green waistcoat.

"A miracle awaits," he proclaimed.

Smiling, the two men headed into the Mission Saloon, where they faced a stern-faced Ophelia.

Fergal leaned on the bar as if nothing was amiss, but Ophelia reached over the counter, took hold of his collar, and dragged him forward so he bellied up to the bar.

"Is there anything you want to say to me?" she muttered.

"I'm sorry?" Fergal suggested, and then gulped when she didn't open her hand. "And I won't give Maria another tonic."

"See that you don't." She opened her hand, releasing Fergal, and then went to the pump, a large smile appearing. "Today my sarsaparillas don't have rye extract, so I'll serve you two doubles with extra foam. Then I'm going to sit with Maria. I expect you to have drunk them when I return."

She provided the promised drinks, along with a warning glare as to what she'd do if they remained untouched, and left them. Without the rye extract, the sarsaparillas had returned to their previous undrinkable state and so they poked at them, pensively, while taking advantage of the prime location to survey what was happening outside.

With the eclipse show ready to begin shortly, people were gravitating toward the edge of town, where Oliver was considering the newly constructed enclosure. He frowned, and then headed across the road to the Mission Saloon instead.

"I thought I should come over and apologize," Oliver said, shuffling from foot to foot in the doorway. "I really did want to help you, but . . ."

"Nobody bears you any ill will for what happened last night, or for helping Woody," Fergal said, beckoning Oliver to come closer. "And to show there's no hard feelings, enjoy a sarsaparilla."

Fergal pushed his drink toward Oliver.

"And mine," Randolph said, matching Fergal's action.

Oliver joined them, his relief evident in his smile. With the two men being so friendly, he sat on a stool and ventured a sip.

"You don't look happy," Fergal said.

"I'm not," Oliver murmured. "I came to study the eclipse, not to discuss with cowpokes whether Sagittarius was a better gunslinger than Orion."

"Then cheer up. The eclipse is soon due and then you can return to your professing."

Oliver chuckled. "Well, I'm not exactly a professor. Woody added that claim to make today's show sound more authoritative."

"Not to worry. I doubt many people around here would know what a professor is." Fergal rubbed his brow. "Me included. But from what I've heard, you know what you're talking about."

"I do, but I'm no professor." Oliver sighed. "Or at least not until after the eclipse, I hope."

"Because," Fergal offered, "you're the only scientist from your university who's come here to see the eclipse, so that gives you an edge?"

"Not quite." Oliver withdrew a watch from his waist-coat to check the time before answering. "Science is mostly theoretical. You can expound theories, and as long as enough scientists are prepared to discuss them, you can build a reputation. You never have to worry about reality intruding. But if your theories aren't popular, reality can help."

"And are your theories not popular?"

"Opinion is divided."

"How divided?"

"Everybody says I'm wrong." Oliver puffed out his chest. "I say I'm right."

"About what?"

Oliver took a long gulp of his drink. When he stopped coughing, he put it down and began gesturing as he explained.

"There's a methodology for predicting the incidence of solar eclipses. The trouble with methods is they can be wrong. I have a new predictive theory, except nobody accepts it. When this eclipse happens at the time and place I've predicted, I can return home a scientific hero, my theories proved and my detractors embarrassed. A professorship won't be far away."

Fergal raised his eyebrows. "I can see you're a deep-thinking man. So I have something you might appreciate seeing."

Oliver glanced at his watch and then nodded.

"All right, but you'll have to be quick. First contact is in ten minutes."

Fergal told Randolph to keep Ophelia occupied if she returned. Then he led Oliver into the back room. The room was empty, but he directed Oliver to the large door set into the floor beside the far wall. He knelt down and threw it open.

"Ophelia's storeroom," he proclaimed.

Steps led downward into darkness. A cold waft of stale air emerged. Oliver stared down into the darkness and furrowed his brow.

"I'm not going in there," he said. "It's dark and cold and damp."

"It is. But you can see everything you need to see from here."

With his hands on his knees, Oliver leaned forward to peer down the steps.

"And what am I looking at?"

Fergal reached down to pat the walls. They returned a solid sound.

"When the Mexican Army commandeered the mission, this building was used as an armory, and so the storeroom's secure and can hold dozens of barrels and crates. It makes a fine storage area."

Oliver narrowed his eyes, seeing farther as his vision became accustomed to the poor light.

"I can see that."

"Except Ophelia hasn't got much need for storage. She has only three barrels in there. So her storeroom is just a large room she keeps open because there's nothing worth stealing. I'll show you the door." Fergal patted the wood, which returned a satisfyingly dense sound. "It's so solid I reckon it could withstand dynamite."

Oliver looked the door up and down. "It's a fine door."

"It is." Fergal slammed the door into the frame with a thud. "But if she were to have something in there she didn't want anyone to steal, she could secure this bolt, turn this lock, and nobody would ever get in."

Fergal rattled the large bolt.

"I'm sure," Oliver said, considering the bolt, "Ophelia must feel secure knowing that."

"I'm sure she does."

For long moments they stood in silence.

"And the reason you showed me this?"

"I thought a scientific man such as yourself would be interested." Fergal patted the door. "So if you want to learn more about the storeroom before you leave, you just have to ask."

Oliver blew out his cheeks as he looked at his watch. "I'll remember that," he said.

"Be sure that you do," Fergal said with a wink.

Chapter Eleven

Thirty minutes after Woody had opened the gate to his enclosure, the townsfolk had filled the available seats. They were smiling and eager, despite the ten dollars a head entrance fee, although the promise of ten times your money back if this wasn't the greatest show ever ensured that everyone was relaxed.

Woody closed the gate and looked around for Hank and Vernon, aiming to tell them to make sure that nobody sneaked in late for free, but both men had disappeared. He shrugged and joined Oliver in the center circle of seats.

Oliver had set up his telescope, a table on which he could write notes, and several smaller pieces of equipment, the use of which Woody didn't dare inquire about. He guessed that if he did, Oliver would explain what they were for, and he didn't fancy the headaches that would induce.

"Are you ready?" he asked.

Oliver glanced up, his face wreathed in the largest smile Woody had seen him provide.

"I am."

"And is the greatest show ever ready?"

Oliver glanced at his watch and then at the sun.

"If my predictions are correct, it is ready."

Woody beamed and then turned to the seated audience. He held his arms aloft, asking for quiet.

"People of Sundown," he shouted, his voice strident. "The new owner of El Hombre is proud to present to you Professor Oliver Rhinehart and his amazing stellar phenomenon. So I give you the greatest show ever. I give you . . . the eclipse."

With a coordinated movement, two hundred heads turned to the sky. They stared at the burning sun for several seconds and then hung their heads, blinking and rubbing their eyes.

"But not just yet," Woody said, rubbing his own watering eyes.

"I am ready to create history," Thaddeus proclaimed, thrusting his cleaned and gleaming sword aloft.

Randolph held out his and Fergal's untouched sarsaparillas.

"Sounds intriguing," he said. "I'd like to see someone down two sarsaparillas."

Thaddeus dismissed Randolph's joking offer with a harsh glare.

"I am not referring to that. Today will be my finest performance."

Fergal looked down the road. Aside from a few impoverished stragglers skulking outside the El Hombre, pretty much everyone in town had gone to Woody's show.

"It's a pity so few will see it," Fergal said.

"That does not matter. Two days ago I performed to nobody and, even if I have to return to performing alone, all that matters is my art. And I will be magnificent!"

With his back straight and his sword resting on a shoulder, Thaddeus paraded out from the Mission Saloon. He swung to a halt in the center of the road where, with his legs planted wide apart, he surveyed his meager audience. He checked on the sun and then knelt and raised a hand.

For a while he emoted incomprehensible Shakespeare. Then he whipped out his sword as the first of the sword fights started under the most dramatic setting possible. And without doubt, the sky did appear to be darker and more dramatic, even if, as Randolph and Fergal reckoned from the Mission Saloon, his acting hadn't improved.

Soon, beyond the edge of town in Woody's enclosure, the darkness became even more tangible, forming an eerie kind of twilight. The temperature was dropping too, making Oliver rub his hands and bat them against his arms.

Standing before the rows of eclipse watchers, Oliver gestured to the sun.

"At this point," he announced, "the moon has nearly covered ninety percent of the sun's surface, and the darkness is deepening with every passing second. We are now less than ten minutes from totality."

Oliver had projected the sun's image onto a card he'd fixed before his telescope. He tucked a stray strand of wispy hair beneath his hat, and then bent to examine the sun's projected image.

With a protractor, he measured the sliver of uncovered sun. He frowned and stood back to scratch his forehead.

He tapped his fingers as he revised his calculations and then narrowed his eyes and stared at the sun's projection. With a steady rhythm, he poked the image with his protractor, but the image didn't change.

The protractor fell from his hand. He paled.

"Anything wrong?" Woody asked.

Oliver straightened and rubbed his brow. "I . . . I . . ."

"No need to panic. The greatest show ever is building nicely."

"I'm a scientist," Oliver said, his voice gruff. "I don't care about that."

"I know, but today science and profit are merging nicely."

Oliver looked at the sun's projection for one final time and then shuffled round to face Woody.

"I have to go."

"Why?"

"Because . . . Because I left some equipment I need for my experiments in the stable."

Woody snorted a rare laugh. "You scientists may know about the sky, but in other ways you are fools. You have had years to prepare for this and then you forget something."

"I've had a lot on my mind recently," Oliver murmured, shuffling away from his telescope.

"Better hurry, then," Woody said, tapping his watch. "You have less than nine minutes."

Oliver nodded and then broke into a run. He hurried past the end block of seats and raised his jacket as he vaulted the enclosure fence. Still with his jacket held high, he scampered down Sundown's main drag.

Woody watched him in bemusement and then joined the crowd in shielding his eyes and taking furtive glances up at the sun. So nobody saw Oliver hurtle past El Hombre. Nor did they see him take a skidding detour to avoid the emoting Thaddeus.

But one thing was certain. Oliver knew where he was going.

In the Mission Saloon, Randolph and Fergal poked their sarsaparillas back and forth across the bar, steeling themselves to imbibe them before Ophelia returned.

As the darkness deepened, their conversation lessened until they sat in silence. Only the occasional whine from Thaddeus' one-man sword fight drifted in to interrupt their thoughts.

Then, behind them, the door crashed back against the wall and footfalls thudded across the saloon. Randolph looked over his shoulder, but nobody was there.

"What was that?" he said, glancing around.

"What was what?" Fergal asked.

"It sounded like someone dashing across the saloon in a hurry."

Fergal shrugged. "Didn't hear nothing."

From within the back store, a door slammed.

"You must have heard that. Someone's in the store-room. Perhaps they're stealing Ophelia's stock."

"Could be." Fergal got to his feet. "I'll check."

Fergal headed into the back room. Inside the saloon, Randolph heard the storeroom door rattle. Then a bolt screeched and a click sounded as the large lock fell into place.

Fergal returned to the saloon shaking his head.

"Anybody there?" Randolph asked.

"Nope." Fergal slipped back on to his stool. "Must have been rats."

Randolph contemplated his drink. "So you locked those rats in then, did you?"

"Yeah. Don't want them scurrying around spoiling our peaceful afternoon."

"This here total eclipse," Tucker Moorhead said to Jim, the man standing next to him in Woody's enclosure.

"Yeah?" Jim said.

"It's supposed to be happening in another two minutes, right?"

"Yup."

"And it'll be the most amazing thing we'll ever see?"

"Yup."

"Did you listen to anything else Oliver said about it last night?"

"Nope. I paid attention when he set fire to your pants and when he showed us that picture of that Comanche felling a buffalo, but I didn't listen when he droned on about the eclipse." Jim glanced around. "For that matter, where is Oliver?"

Tucker followed Jim's gaze and shrugged.

"Don't know. Perhaps he's experimenting somewhere."

"So what were you going to ask me about this here total eclipse?"

"Well, from the bits of Oliver's lecture I listened to, it gets darker and darker until it's as dark as night. Is that so?"

"Yeah. I reckon it gets mighty dark."

"That's what I thought." Tucker put a hand to his brow as he considered the sky. "Except I reckon it's getting lighter."

"Anything happening out there?" Randolph asked from the bar.

Fergal looked out the window. Thaddeus was kneeling

again, a hand raised to the sun, loudly imploring it to do something or other. His sword was stuck downward between his arm and his chest, showing he'd just been killed and he was making an impassioned last speech. Unfortunately, it was so impassioned the sword toppled over, but that didn't put Thaddeus off; he continued to bleat.

"Not much that I can see," Fergal said.

Randolph put a hand to his ear. "Is that Thaddeus shouting and screaming?"

"It was him before, but that noise isn't loud enough to be him." Fergal went to the door. He peered outside and down the road and then returned to the bar. "Sorry, I couldn't see who was making the noise on account of this huge, angry mob brandishing their fists and blocking the road."

Randolph nodded. "Is this huge, angry mob heading in any particular direction?"

"El Hombre."

"You reckon we should investigate?"

"No." Fergal picked up his drink. "I reckon we should have another go at drinking our sarsaparillas. That'll give that huge angry mob enough time to move out of the way."

Chapter Twelve

P arting will be a sweet sorrow," Thaddeus proclaimed, brandishing his sword at Woody when his arrival interrupted his performance, "when you're waving good-bye to your head."

Thaddeus' threat made Woody skid to a halt. With the enraged mob closing in from behind and the irate Thaddeus standing before him, Woody looked around for another escape route. El Hombre was the only option, but by the time he reached the boardwalk, it was already too late. Numerous people had blocked his route into his saloon, and now the mob was spreading out to surround him.

"What happened to the eclipse?" Tucker Moorhead demanded, slamming his hands on his hips.

"It must have missed us," Woody offered.

"But you said it'd be the most amazing thing we'd ever see."

Woody rolled his shoulders and stood tall, regaining some of his usual composure.

"Oliver Rhinehart said that and he was wrong. I am just as surprised as you are."

"But you promised us our money back if we weren't happy." Tucker looked around, receiving a chorus of encouragement. "And we're not happy!"

"Like I said, you will get your money back," Woody said. "The eclipse fell short of being the greatest show ever."

"But you said we'd get it back tenfold."

This demand received a chorus of nods from the enraged crowd.

"Perhaps I did." Woody spread his hands and smiled. "But I am as disappointed as you are. You wouldn't want to hold me to that rash promise, would you?"

Tucker stood defiantly, but Woody's piercing gaze knocked some of the fight out of him, and so he started to shake his head. Then a cry went up from the back of the crowd.

"Tenfold," a voice shouted. "You promised tenfold."

Woody peered over everyone's head to see Randolph and Fergal standing outside the Mission Saloon with their hands around their mouths, bellowing their demand.

"Yeah, you promised tenfold," Tucker shouted. "Tenfold. Tenfold. Tenfold!"

More voices echoed the cry, the volume growing with every chant.

Woody shouted something back, but the chanting

drowned out his offer. As one, the crowd stepped forward, its indignation growing. Woody backed away, but he slammed into a post.

The crowd took another pace, making him try to backtrack, but he only succeeded in backing himself up the pole. Now everyone had joined in the chant and they'd raised their fists.

Woody was searching for an avenue of escape when his gaze fell on the opening swinging doors of the El Hombre. Vernon Black peered out to consider the crowd, and then said something to someone inside, presumably Hank Kelly, but Woody caught his attention with a frantic wave.

"Help," he said simply.

Vernon jerked back and forth, his attention shifting from inside the saloon to Woody and then back to the saloon where, judging by his eager expression, something interesting was happening. With an apologetic shrug, he headed outside and paced down the boardwalk to join Woody.

He rolled his shoulders and bunched his sizeable fists as he considered the advancing mob.

"What kind of help are you interested in?" he asked.

Woody rubbed his sweating brow. "I will give you one hundred dollars to get me out of here."

"It's a deal." Vernon considered the nearest irate chanting person. "But it'll cost you five hundred to get you out of here alive."

"I am not paying—" Woody ducked. A rock flew over his head and cannoned into the post, spraying splinters over his shoulders. "Deal."

Vernon stood before Woody with his arms folded. He glared at the mob, casting his stern gaze across the crowd until it fell on one man, Tucker. Tucker was chanting, but Vernon's glare silenced him and made him shuffle backward a pace.

Vernon moved his gaze on to the next man and ran a finger along his gun belt. That man silenced and edged back a pace too.

Person by person, a zone of calm grew in all directions, as Vernon's glare silenced the mob. When sufficient quiet had descended, Woody stepped out from behind Vernon.

"Now that you have stopped chanting," he said, "we can reach a compromise. The person you should be annoyed with is Oliver Rhinehart. I suggest we find him and demand to know what happened to the eclipse. Then I will refund everyone's money and we will have the eclipse party I had promised. But this time, the drinks are on El Hombre!"

Everyone cheered. Outside the Mission Saloon, Fergal and Randolph tried to start a new chant of "Tenfold," but the crowd's cheering drowned their cries and the enthusiasm for a riot petered out.

"So does anyone know where Oliver went?" Woody said.

"I haven't seen him," Tucker said helpfully. "But he was staying in the mission stable. I reckon you should start looking there."

The crowd turned and all eyes alighted on Randolph and Fergal. The collective gazes of two hundred people made both men shuffle backward a guilty pace.

"Fergal has him," Woody muttered.

As one, the crowd took a pace toward them. In unison, Randolph and Fergal backed away a pace. The crowd advanced another pace.

With the situation looking desperate, Randolph searched for an escape route. As far as he could work out, a frantic dash to the stable, followed by an even more frantic dash out of town, was the only option. But just as he was about to catch Fergal's eye, the swinging doors of the El Hombre crashed open.

The crowd swiveled round to face the saloon, and they were confronted by the sight of Hank Kelly dashing out with a bulging saddlebag over his shoulder, presumably containing the contents of the saloon's safe.

On the run, his gaze sought out Vernon, who moved toward him and then stopped. He looked at Hank and then at Woody. With a shrug, he decided that the already earned reward of five hundred dollars was more tempting than the possibility of getting away with the stolen money. He rejoined Woody.

"Stop him!" Woody shouted. "He has my money. I cannot refund anyone without it."

This comment mobilized the crowd and they advanced on Hank, blocking his route to his horse. Hank tore his gun from its holster and aimed it at the nearest man, who thrust his hands above his head, but many in the crowd still edged toward him.

He looked around until he saw a row of horses tethered outside the bank on the Mission Saloon side of town. He hurried to them. Brandishing his gun made the people before him peel away, but trapped in the center of the crowd stood Ophelia and, as everyone hurried away from her, she was knocked to her knees.

She moved to get up, but found that Hank was looming over her. With a sly grin, he grabbed her shoulders, dragged her to her feet, and then swung her round to place her between himself and the crowd.

"I've got all the cover I need here," he muttered. "Now, let me leave town or I shoot the woman."

Hank pressed the barrel of his gun to Ophelia's temple. Ophelia struggled, but on finding that Hank had a firm grip, she went limp.

The crowd stopped advancing and backed away. Many raised their hands, showing they wouldn't intervene.

Hank nodded approvingly and then set his jaw firm as he dragged Ophelia toward the nearest horse.

"Unhand her, you cowardly knave," a voice demanded from the back of the crowd.

Everybody looked around to see who had spoken. With a coordinated scurry of feet, the crowd parted.

Standing in the gap was Thaddeus. He had adopted his heroic actor pose, a leg thrust out, a hand held aloft. In the other hand, he clutched his gleaming sword.

Hank snorted as he backed away another pace.

"I'm not listening to a man wearing tights," he said.

Thaddeus flourished his sword. "Then you will feel the kiss of hard steel."

Hank tightened his grip on Ophelia's shoulders and pulled her up on her tiptoes. He chuckled without mirth.

"A man with a sword shouldn't threaten a man with a gun."

Undaunted, Thaddeus took a pace toward Hank and then stood sideways. He raised an arched hand behind him and aimed the sword at Hank.

"Don't . . . do it . . . Thaddeus," Ophelia said, between gasps.

"A hero must act," Thaddeus proclaimed, "and an actor must be a hero."

Hank glared at him. Then, with a snort of derision, he pushed Ophelia away for her to fall to her knees at his feet.

The crowd backed away, giving the two men sufficient room for their showdown. Everybody standing behind Thaddeus quickly took up other positions.

In the center of the road, Hank spat on the ground as he edged his gun away from Ophelia and toward Thaddeus. In retaliation, Thaddeus delivered a rousing upward thrust of his sword. But it slipped from his grip and flew from his hand.

The sword turned end-over-end as it hurtled toward the brightening sun. As one, the crowd craned their necks, watching the sword swing up into the sky, the blade dazzling.

The sword reached its zenith, slowed to a halt, and then seemed to be frozen for a moment, dangling bright and shining against the sky.

Then it headed earthward.

Hank stared up at the sword, entranced, before realizing in horror where it was heading. He dived to the ground, but he was too late.

The sword reached its inevitable destination.

A collective groan arose from the watching crowd. Everyone turned away, wincing.

Fergal nudged Randolph. "That just had to hurt."

"Yeah," Randolph said. "That man won't ever get through a door again."

Thaddeus hurried to Ophelia's side. He ran a finger along his moustache and arched an eyebrow, as he drew her to her feet, while Woody pushed through the crowd and checked on Hank. Confirming that a man pinned to the ground with a three-foot sword wasn't in the best of health, he picked up the saddlebag.

He looked inside to confirm that bills filled the bag to overflowing and then smiled, but when he looked up, it was to face the crowd.

The sight of the bag of money drove all other thoughts away, and despite Vernon's hulking presence, every one of them had a refund on their minds.

As ever, Tucker was at the front of the queue.

Chapter Thirteen

We have to hide," Randolph said, when he was sure that Ophelia had escaped from her ordeal unscathed.

"The chapel will do," Fergal said. "I don't reckon Woody will go in there."

Randolph nodded. After taking the opportunity to give Ophelia and Thaddeus their sarsaparillas to revive their spirits, they left them in the Mission Saloon.

Outside, the refunded crowd was dispersing. There was no sign of Woody, so they hurried around the saloon, aiming to go to the chapel. They'd managed only a few paces when they skidded to a halt.

Woody was waiting for them.

"I have now paid out every cent I owned to that mob," he said.

Fergal set his hands on his hips. "I believe the truth is you have paid out every cent that Sydney Grant owned."

"That is not a relevant matter. What is relevant is the fact that you organized that mob."

Fergal spread his hands. "How could we have done that from inside the Mission Saloon?"

Woody smiled and cocked his head to one side, defying Fergal to acknowledge that, when it came to being devious, they were both as bad as each other.

"I don't know how you did it, but somehow you knew Oliver had miscalculated about the eclipse. Somehow you knew there would be a riot outside El Hombre, so you stationed that actor there to block my way. And somehow you even knew Hank was planning to steal the contents of Sydney Grant's safe."

Fergal hadn't been aware of the last element, but he accepted this assessment with a nod.

"And that is the difference between us, and why you made a big mistake when you turned against me. I think ahead. You do not."

"I am the one with the clearer vision." Woody provided a cold smile. "But today I will settle for having the faster gun."

He clicked his fingers and Vernon stepped out from behind the saloon.

Fergal and Randolph glanced at each other and smiled.

"You can settle for that," Fergal said, "but today we'll settle for having the faster feet."

Woody opened his mouth to ask what he meant, but before he could speak, Randolph and Fergal broke into a run. Neither man looked back as they skirted around heaps of rubble and vaulted rocks in their path. Years of running from trouble had taught them that, when running, they should just keep going, so neither man looked back even after they'd hurtled into the chapel.

Only when they were in danger of running into Bishop Finnegan did they skid to a halt.

"We were eager to get to your final service," Randolph said, smiling.

"I am pleased you have come," Finnegan said, eyeing them dubiously. "My final sermon will take inspiration from the events here. It will concentrate on the evils of liquor, lying, and any of your other misdemeanors that I can think of."

Both men provided humble bows. Then they sat in the same positions as they had done yesterday. As they had hoped, Woody didn't follow them in.

They waited patiently and presently a familiar scraping sounded.

They turned to watch Ophelia maneuvering Maria into the chapel. Thaddeus was at her shoulder, still clutching his sword, and looking pleased with himself after his brave act. Ophelia drew the bed up to its usual position and, with Ophelia sitting on one side of the aisle and Thaddeus on the other, they too awaited Finnegan's final service in the Mission Santa Maria.

"Woody and his new hired gun will be waiting to get

us the moment we come out," Randolph whispered to Fergal from the corner of his mouth. "So let's hope this is a long service."

"Agreed," Fergal said. "Perhaps we might even get sanctuary afterward."

"We won't. Finnegan is leaving after the service."

"I'm still hoping for a miracle and that he changes his mind."

Randolph swirled round to look at him. "I thought your talk of miracles had to do with us beating Woody. What have you got planned in that devious little mind of yours?"

Fergal winced. "It might be best if you wait and see."

Randolph slapped a hand down on Fergal's arm.

"Tell me now. It'll give me a chance to get used to the idea." Randolph waited, but Fergal sat with pursed lips. "Then tell me this: does this plan cross the line?"

Fergal coughed, and then cast Randolph an ashamed look. "It does."

"By how much?"

"Well, let's say this is the line." Fergal raised a hand. "Then this miracle will be . . ." Fergal moved his other hand until he'd stretched his arm out.

"That bad?"

"Worse. I reckon my hand should be out at Shinbone."

Randolph flopped back in his chair, sighing, but before he could ask for more details, Finnegan made his way to the front.

He faced the small congregation and folded his hands into his robes.

"Regrettably, this is to be the last time anyone will stand before a congregation in the Mission Santa Maria. Today's events have provided final proof that my decision was the right one. Riots, robberies, showdowns . . . Sundown is just too dangerous a place for the mission, but before I begin I would like to—"

"Before you speak," Fergal said, standing, "I need to say that this shouldn't be the last time."

While Finnegan bristled, Ophelia offered him a resigned smile.

"I welcome your support," she said, "however misguided it is, but Bishop Finnegan has made his decision. My time here is over. Maria's time here is over. The mission's time is over."

"But the mission is needed."

"It is, but not by enough people."

Fergal provided his most honest smile and lowered his voice to a comforting tone.

"Not everyone who needs the mission can be here every day. People are spread thin and wide around these parts."

At this comment, Finnegan provided a small nod, accepting that for once he'd made a good point.

"Yes, but . . . ," Ophelia murmured, but then trailed off when a noise sounded outside the door.

Randolph swirled round, worried that Woody and

Vernon had decided to confront them now, but he was surprised to see a familiar face. Jim Reed, the man who had heckled them a few days ago in Shinbone, was standing in the doorway.

Ophelia wasted no time in encouraging him to come inside, but Finnegan spoke up.

"Anyone attending this service will not get free whiskey," he proclaimed.

Jim shook his head. "We don't want that."

He looked outside and beckoned. Others entered.

Randolph recognized several of the people as being among the disgruntled crowd in Shinbone, and he was sure he'd seen others in similar crowds in similar towns where they'd failed to sell bottles of Fergal's tonic.

He leaned toward Fergal as the procession of people filed into seats, each person stopping beside Maria to murmur a few words.

"That's where you went last night," he said. "You rounded up all the people who believed Maria had helped them."

"I got the word out," Fergal said, proudly.

"Then you did a good thing. That's sure not to have crossed the line."

Fergal winced, suggesting this wasn't the matter that had worried him, but Randolph didn't get to question him as, with the chapel now full, the delighted Finnegan called for quiet.

He cast his benign gaze over his congregation. So many people were inside the chapel that most had to stand, but everybody appeared content.

That approval continued as Finnegan provided a fuller service than the one he'd delivered last night. This especially delighted Randolph, as it lengthened the time before they'd have to go outside and face Woody and Vernon.

The previous eerie twilight had receded and the day returned to full light by the time the service ended.

"That was a good service," Ophelia said, when she joined Finnegan at the front.

"It was good to see so many here," Finnegan said, addressing the new and unexpected arrivals. "And you all came for the right reason."

"We had to come," Jim said.

"Maria has done so much for us," another said.

"Yes. Don't take her away."

"We need the mission."

"We really do."

Finnegan rubbed his jaw. "Is that because you believe Maria has performed miracles?"

Several people shuffled in their seats and Randolph wasn't surprised when Jim stepped forward.

"I heard that she cured an attack of boils," he declared, as he made his way through the chapel to reach the front.

"Is that so?" Finnegan asked, his tone lowering.

Jim nodded and then waited until everyone was looking at him before stating his case.

"I have heard of many people who have been cured of ailments after seeing her." People looked at the sleeping Maria, but he raised a hand, drawing everyone's attention back to him. "But she has something more important than that to offer."

He paused with his hand held aloft, his silence making everyone edge forward, eager to hear what he would say.

"What is it?" Finnegan said.

"It is this." Jim turned to the bishop. "Seeing her quiet struggle against her plight helped us in ways that touched us more than the physical changes did. It's a long way to come, but when we do, it gives us heart and hope. Please don't abandon the mission."

This statement made Finnegan raise his eyebrows.

"You are right that the distances you have to travel are great and it is not always possible to fill the chapel . . ." He looked around, nodding. "I need to think on this some more."

He called Ophelia over and they walked beyond the altar, where they talked in low voices. Everyone watched them, their concerned expressions registering their hope. Accordingly, Randolph leaned toward Fergal.

"We might be getting that miracle we hoped for after all," he said.

"We might," Fergal murmured, watching Ophelia and Finnegan with consternation, "unless I can stop it."

He moved to rise, but Randolph grabbed his arm.

"Stop it? Why would you want to do that?"

"Because it looks as if Finnegan is about to change his mind without my . . . my intervention." Fergal struggled to extricate his arm. "Unless I stop it, he might change his mind back again."

"What do we need to do?"

Fergal opened his mouth to reply, but before he could speak, a cry went up from behind. Randolph swirled round to find that Ophelia had returned to the congregation and was staring at the empty bed in the aisle with a hand to her mouth.

"She's gone," she shouted. "Maria's gone!"

Everyone looked around the chapel, confirming she wasn't inside. Their perusal ended with them all facing the open doorway. Jim sprinted to reach the door first. He peered outside, and then came to a sudden halt.

Within the chapel, Fergal lowered his head.

"Too late," he murmured.

Randolph looked at him, then at Jim, and then at the empty bed, wondering what Fergal had done, but he got his answer when Jim pointed outside with a shaking hand.

"Look," he cried. "It's a miracle!"

Chapter Fourteen

W hat have you done, Fergal?" Randolph asked, shaking Fergal's shoulder, but he got no answer other than a pained bleat and a shamefaced stare at the floor.

So Randolph joined the others, craning his neck and trying to see what had interested them outside. Too many people were in his way, but thankfully they were all nudging their way out. And from their gasps of surprise as they emerged, whatever it was, it was amazing.

Randolph was between Bishop Finnegan and Ophelia as they slipped outside, and so he heard their gasps of awe a moment before he saw what was happening.

Despite Fergal's warning, his heart pounded and his mouth fell open in wonder.

Fergal had cured Maria.

Twenty yards from the chapel, a cloaked young woman with her hood drawn down to cover her lowered face was standing before them. She was the same build as Maria and, aside from the cloak, she was wearing the same clothes. But what confirmed that she had to be Maria was the long hair that emerged from her hood and cascaded down to her waist.

Everyone stood rooted to the spot, watching this unexpected apparition.

"Maria?" Ophelia murmured, moving forward. Her motion encouraged others to edge toward the newly awakened Maria, but from the back of the crowd, Finnegan spoke up.

"Let me speak to her," he said.

He placed a comforting hand on Ophelia's shoulder and then set off, parting the people like a stick drawn through water as he made his stately progress toward her.

Maria looked up, although the strong sunlight kept her face in shadow. She made a sign with her right hand, perhaps a blessing. Then she turned and headed toward the Mission Saloon.

"Wait!" Ophelia cried, breaking into a run.

She hurried on to go past Finnegan, but he took her arm as she passed.

"We mustn't crowd her," he said. "After such a long sleep, seeing all these people must be a shock. I will speak with her first."

Ophelia gave a small nod, but when Finnegan set off, she still followed on behind, as did the rest of the crowd.

Maria had a forty-yard lead on them, but when she reached the back of the saloon, she tried to climb over a heap of rubble and stumbled. A concerned cry went up from the watchers, and despite Finnegan's plea, everyone surged forward to help her.

Marla leaped to her feet, again stumbling on the loose rocks, and the motion let her look back at the approaching people who were all advancing at speed.

She took flight. She scampered over the rest of the rocks and then made a smart right turn and disappeared from view around the saloon.

The crowd came to a halt. Her sudden disappearance surprised everyone as much as her sudden arrival had. Finnegan was the first to react. He ordered everyone to split up and head across the quadrangle, thereby cutting her off from two separate directions, while he and Ophelia went to the saloon.

Randolph watched the frenetic activity and decided that he didn't need to help; enough people were going in search of her. Besides, he needed to talk to Fergal.

When he returned to the chapel he found him in the same position as he'd left him, facing front with his head in his hands. Randolph took a deep breath and joined him.

They sat quietly for a minute until the sounds of the pursuing crowd had receded. Then Fergal looked at him and offered a tentative smile.

"Tell me," Randolph asked, still unsure about what he'd seen, "how did you cure Maria?"

Fergal winced. "I tried. I really did."

Randolph looked aloft as he composed himself.

"That means I should have asked: was that Maria?" He watched Fergal shake his head. "So what have you done with her?"

"She's fine, if that's what you're asking. They'll find her before long."

Randolph gripped Fergal's forearm. "Fergal, what's happening?"

Fergal gulped and when he spoke his voice caught several times.

"While Jim was presenting his case, nobody was looking at Maria. Two men took her outside. Then Jim's long-haired daughter provided that miracle."

"Why?"

"For ten dollars. Jim wanted more but I—"

"I didn't mean that. I meant why did you do such a terrible thing?"

Fergal shrugged. "I thought it would make Bishop Finnegan believe he'd seen a miracle and keep the mission open."

"That was wrong, Fergal."

"I know, but it felt like the right thing to do last night. It doesn't feel so good now that Finnegan was ready to change his mind without the miracle, but hopefully nobody will find Jim's daughter and work out what happened."

"Yeah," Randolph said, unable to keep the bitterness from his voice. "Let's hope they don't find her, so Ophelia will only have to wonder why Maria has gone back to sleep."

Fergal opened his mouth to reply, but as nothing he could say would excuse his actions, he said nothing and lowered his head.

They sat quietly, awaiting the pronouncement on the miracle. They didn't have to wait long, although Randolph was surprised that the first person to return was Thaddeus.

"I am very angry," Thaddeus announced from the doorway. "And this time I'm not acting."

Randolph considered his flaring eyes, his belligerent feet-apart stance, his clenched left fist, and his recently cleaned sword resting on his right shoulder.

"I know," he said. "You're not that good an actor."

"I will let that insult pass while I have other insults to deal with."

Thaddeus paced inside, heading for them, pushing and kicking chairs aside to clear a path until he was standing before them.

"What's the problem?" Fergal said innocently.

"This is." Thaddeus pointed to the door with his sword, and with the impeccable timing that he'd never been able to manage onstage, Ophelia appeared in the doorway. At her side was Finnegan, and in his arms, the sleeping form of Maria.

With Fergal not saying anything in his defense, Randolph tried his own innocent smile.

"So Maria fell asleep again," he murmured, although his surprise didn't sound convincing, even to his own ears.

"She has," Thaddeus boomed. "Do you have anything to say about that?"

Randolph gulped to clear his suddenly dry throat, and then stood to confront Thaddeus.

"Tell me what happened."

Thaddeus searched his eyes, presumably looking for signs that he already knew the truth, before he replied.

"We found Maria in the saloon, lying beside the bar. The others are still searching for the miraculous young woman who appeared before us."

"They will be disappointed," Randolph said, "when they find out she's gone back to sleep."

"They will, but not when they hear the full account of what we saw."

Thaddeus flared his eyes, defying Randolph to ask for more details, but it was Finnegan who completed the story.

"Only we saw that there were in fact two young women. The one we thought was Maria was with two men. They ran away from the saloon, leaving us to find the real Maria after they'd perpetrated this cruel, elaborate, but ultimately inept hoax."

"And I know who organized it," Thaddeus continued. "The man who asked me about stagecraft last night, the man who asked me to perform outside in the road when a riot erupted around me."

"He was trying to help your performance," Randolph said.

Thaddeus uttered a theatrical snort, but Fergal stood, sighed, and then shuffled round to stand beside Randolph.

"You don't have to speak on my behalf, Randolph," he said. "This time I have to explain myself."

Thaddeus bristled with indignation.

"You will do more than explain. You have treated me with contempt, offended a good lady and her charge, and jeopardized the future of this mission. There's only one answer to that." Thaddeus swung the sword round to brandish it beneath Fergal's chin. "You will suffer the same fate as Hank Kelly did."

"Now just you—" Randolph began, but Fergal pushed him aside. Then, when his gesture moved him dangerously close to the sword, he gulped and sidestepped it.

"Stand back, Randolph. This is my problem. I crossed the line. I'll deal with him." Fergal rolled his scrawny shoulders. "And pass me your gun. I reckon I'll need it."

"But you've never used a gun," Randolph said.

"Then, in this case, gun against sword will be a fair fight."

As Randolph and Fergal stared at each, Finnegan placed Maria down on her bed and then gestured at them.

"This is a place of worship," he said. "You will not fight in here."

"It will not take me long," Thaddeus proclaimed, "to make this man regret his tawdry tricks."

Finnegan continued to complain, but with a swish of his sword, Thaddeus advanced on Fergal, making him scramble away.

Fergal shot Randolph's holster an imploring glance, and seeing that Fergal was determined in this matter, Randolph slipped his gun from its holster and under-handed it to him.

The gun smacked into Fergal's stomach, his waving hands missing it by some distance, and it clattered to the floor. With Thaddeus continuing to advance, Fergal dropped to one knee and picked up the gun, and then walked crablike to a position where he could stand.

He swirled round to face the advancing Thaddeus.

"Any advice, Randolph?" he shouted.

"Cock the gun."

"Right. Anything else?"

"Aim it at him . . ." Randolph thought for a moment. "And pull the trigger."

"This is easier than I thought," Fergal said with mis-guided optimism.

Fergal moved to ratchet the Peacemaker, but with his attention on the weapon, Thaddeus had enough time to reach him. He swung the sword around in a brutal swipe that would have cut Fergal in two if it had connected.

But luckily, in desperation, Fergal threw up his gun hand. The barrel of the gun met the sword, and held.

Fergal planted his feet firmly on the floor and, with the weapons locked, they both strained. Randolph glanced at Finnegan, wondering if he would intervene, but he had joined Ophelia kneeling in prayer.

The fighting twosome continued straining, until with a wrench, the weapons parted. Thaddeus had been straining the hardest, and when they released, he rocked to the side, leaving his stomach exposed. Fergal must have been so taken with the swordplay that he lunged in with the gun as if it were a sword and jabbed the barrel into Thaddeus' stomach.

Fergal danced back, smiling at his success, and then sighed and cast an ashamed look at Randolph.

"This is why," Randolph muttered, "I leave you to do the thinking while I use the gun."

"In which case," Fergal said, backing away and trying again to ratchet the gun, "it's your turn to do the thinking."

"You wouldn't be in this mess if I'd have done . . ." Randolph trailed off, figuring that Fergal didn't need criticism when he was fighting for his life.

Thaddeus rubbed his stomach ruefully and then advanced on Fergal, looking for an opening while backing him into the wall.

For his part, the nervous Fergal continued to struggle

with the simple act of cocking the gun, and so Thaddeus lunged in. Fergal scrambled out of the way, toppling several chairs in the process and blocking Thaddeus' path.

"Stand and fight," Thaddeus roared, kicking the chairs out of the way. But when the strewn furniture crashed to the floor close to Maria's bed, Ophelia stood before the bed to protect her, while Finnegan nodded toward the door.

"Perhaps," he said, "I should take her outside."

"Please do," Ophelia said. "She doesn't like the noise."

"How can you tell?" Finnegan asked.

"I just can."

Randolph nodded, remembering how Ophelia had said she'd seen Maria react even if others hadn't, and this made him look at her, wondering if he too could tell that she didn't like the noise.

He watched Finnegan put a hand to the bed as Thaddeus boomed another threat. Then he noticed something . . .

He flinched, not understanding for a moment what he'd seen, but as Thaddeus continued to bellow taunts at Fergal, an idea hit him so hard he stumbled.

He looked at Fergal, who had now cocked the gun, but he was having trouble aiming it while he was busy backing away faster than Thaddeus could advance. Finally Fergal slammed into the wall. He looked right, then left, then chose his direction and sidled along, but all the time Thaddeus closed, swinging the sword back and forth.

"Fergal," Randolph shouted. "Shoot!"

"I . . . I will," Fergal murmured. "I'm just not used to this."

"Don't aim at him. Thrust your arm straight up and fire and fire again."

"Why should I—?"

"Just do it!"

Randolph's voice was so loud that it echoed in the chapel, and despite the apparent stupidity of his demand, this was at least something Fergal could do easily.

He jerked his head away from the gun, thrust his arm straight up, and fired. Then, finding that he'd done that successfully, he blasted again and again.

The lead hammered skyward and clattered into the remnants of the roof above, filling the chapel with the peel of echoing gunfire. Dust and flakes of stone rained down on him, but he continued to fire until his finger twitches produced only silence.

This bizarre behavior made Thaddeus stop advancing and stare at him, but Fergal ignored him and looked past his shoulder, now seeing what Randolph had seen.

"Is that . . . ?" he murmured.

"It sure is," Randolph said, hurrying across the chapel.

"What do I do now?"

"Reload and fire again."

Fergal shot him a glance that said he didn't have any bullets. But then he had a bigger problem to contend with, as Thaddeus took advantage of his lack of fire-power and thrust his sword straight out and aimed it at Fergal's chest, advancing with menacing determination.

Fergal backed away, but he quickly found himself stuck in the corner of the chapel.

As Thaddeus blocked Fergal's escape routes, Randolph hurried past the bed that Finnegan was dragging toward the door. Thaddeus rolled his shoulders and thrust the sword up under Fergal's chin.

"Do you have anything to say before I run you through?" he demanded.

"Yeah," Fergal said with defiance as he stood on tiptoe. "You're a terrible actor."

"As last lines go, that is not memorable." Thaddeus raised his eyebrows. "I have heard it said before."

Thaddeus firmed his shoulders, ready to impale Fergal, but found his arm slapped downward, as Randolph reached him and pushed the sword away. Thaddeus rounded on Randolph and walked into a fierce uppercut to the chin that felled him.

Randolph and Fergal looked at each other and nodded. Then, without comment, Fergal passed over the gun.

Randolph punched in bullets, as he walked back across the chapel, completing the action when he reached Finnegan. He removed Finnegan's hands from the bed and then waited while Fergal dragged the protesting bishop away. Then he raised the gun and aimed it at a point a foot above Maria's head.

"Have you gone mad?" Finnegan demanded.

"Don't shoot her," Ophelia murmured.

"I'm not shooting her," Randolph said, and then fired.

His first shot winged over Maria's head and clattered into the side of the doorway before ricocheting away.

As the noise this generated was minimal, he moved to the side and fired again. This time the bullet whistled so close to her head it kicked splinters from the headrest before pinging into the base of the wall. The smell of cordite grew as he fired repeatedly. Smoke drifted up, blurring his vision. Only when the last echo was dying from the sixth shot did Finnegan manage to shake off Fergal and move over to Randolph, raising a hand.

"I don't know why you're doing this," he said, "but you will stop it."

"I have to carry on," Randolph said, moving to reload the gun.

"You don't," Ophelia screeched. "You have to stop making so much noise."

Randolph opened his mouth to continue arguing, but then another voice spoke up.

"Yes," it said. "Please stop the noise."

The voice was low and weak, and even though Randolph had been hoping to hear it, the plea made him sigh.

Ophelia and Finnegan looked at each other, wondering who had spoken. Together, they looked down at Maria to find she was looking up at them.

"Did . . . did you speak?" Ophelia murmured.

"Only to ask you to stop the gunfire," Maria croaked. "I hate that noise."

Chapter Fifteen

After Maria's first words in two years, the people standing around her didn't react for a length of time that felt almost as long.

Ophelia even looked accusingly at Fergal, as if this was another one of his tricks, but it was left for Randolph to explain.

"When the bandits killed the nuns, she went away somewhere quiet in her mind to avoid the gunfire," he said. "For the last two years, you've shown her only kindness and that gave her no reason to come back. It was a horrible thing to do, but making her live through the noise and the smoke and the gunfire again brought her back."

Randolph noticed that since her statement, Maria had closed her eyes and so he again punched in bullets.

This time nobody complained when he stood by her bed and fired up into the roof. The deafening roar echoed around them, and even on the first shot, Maria waved weakly at him, murmuring at him to be quiet, but he continued to fire.

Only when he'd fired another six times did he stand back. By now Maria was looking around.

"Where is everybody?" she asked. "Why am I in bed?"

"It's a long story," Bishop Finnegan said, kneeling by the bed.

"It's a . . ." Ophelia knelt at her side and then looked up at Fergal and Randolph. "It's a miracle, that's what it is."

"It's not," Finnegan said, taking Maria's limp hand. "It's just the good that even the most misguided people can sometimes do."

As Maria continued to ask questions, Thaddeus joined them, his sword held low as he felt his jaw.

"You appear to have redeemed yourself," he said, looking at Fergal.

"Then hopefully our problem is over," Fergal said.

"For you it is," Thaddeus said, "but not for me. After besmirching your good name, I am now indebted to you. I must repay that debt by dealing with the men who aim to do you harm."

With that comment, Thaddeus tipped the sword to his nose in salute and stalked from the chapel, trying manfully to staunch the blood flow.

"You reckon he's got any chance against Vernon?" Randolph asked.

"Nope," Fergal said, rubbing his hands. "So that's even more good news."

Bishop Finnegan stood outside the chapel looking at the setting sun. He cast his gaze over the near-derelict mission buildings before he turned to Ophelia to give her his final decision.

"Walk with me," he said. "Maria will be fine with Fergal and Randolph and, as I have to leave soon, I need to tell you something."

"What is it?" Ophelia said cautiously.

Finnegan remained silent as they walked to the stable, his lowered head suggesting he was composing what he would say. He stopped in the doorway and considered the few horses there, along with Fergal and Woody's wagons and Ophelia's buggy.

"Maria and you can stay here," he said, turning to her. "I will recommend that we maintain the mission and that a new padre is appointed." He patted the crumbling stable wall. "In fact, as the mission is clearly needed, we need to return this special place to its former glory."

Ophelia's eyes opened wide with surprise. She stuttered, trying to find the right words and settled for a simple declaration.

"Thank you, Your Excellency."

"Now go and tell Maria the good news before I leave for Shinbone."

Ophelia walked away at a dignified pace, but after a dozen strides she gave up trying to appear calm and broke into a run. Finnegan watched her until she went into the chapel, and then turned with a smile on his lips.

He started, finding that Woody was standing behind him, having arrived unheard.

"You and your companion are being searched for," Finnegan said.

"I know," Woody said, unperturbed. "Thaddeus has already frightened off Vernon, and now with all my money gone, I have no reason to stay."

"You are still welcome here. The mission is to remain open."

"That does not interest me." Woody dismissed the matter with a wave. "I will go back to traveling from town to town displaying my attraction."

Finnegan frowned. "I never got to see your attraction. What is it?"

Woody gestured to his wagon. "It is the Treasure of Saint Woody."

Finnegan waited to see if Woody was joking, but when he maintained his firm jaw, he smiled.

"I must admit I'm intrigued by this treasure of a saint who doesn't exist."

Woody provided an icy smile. "Then I will be pleased to show you."

Woody walked over to his wagon, where he helped

Finnegan up onto the back. The bishop stared at the casket, the only item there. He moved around it to consider the object from different angles.

"And where is this treasure?" he asked.

Woody positioned Finnegan before the casket. Then he moved in and twirled the circles on the lid. He extracted a coin from his pocket and raised it for Finnegan to see, and then inserted it into a slot on the lid. He stood back to be at Finnegan's shoulder.

"Just wait," he whispered. "If you are lucky, you may even get the keys to heaven itself."

The coin rattled as it took a complex route around the sides of the casket. Then a hollow clunk sounded as the coin stopped moving. A moment later, the lid jerked up an inch.

As Finnegan edged forward, murmuring with interest, Woody moved in and swung the lid back to let him see inside, but from his position, Finnegan could see only a red glow emanating from within.

Despite his skepticism the light emerging from the casket intrigued him. It played over his face, making him feel warmer, until the light became so bright it dazzled him. He blinked to clear his vision, but his sight remained blurred. He moved in and rested a hand on the rim and then narrowed his eyes as he looked down into the casket.

Through the dazzling light, he detected movement, so he edged to the side to view the casket from a different angle. The moving object suddenly sped up and, unbidden, Finnegan flinched away from it. A glancing blow hit him behind the ear and shoved him forward.

A cry escaped Woody's lips as he slipped and bumped into him. This made Finnegan fall and, although his senses had been jarred, he had the feeling that Woody fell with him.

His shoulder collided with the casket rim. He rebounded and then rolled away to land on the base of the wagon beside the casket. His vision dimmed and his limbs refused to obey, but he remained conscious enough to hear a clatter as Woody hit something solid.

A thud sounded as the casket lid closed.

Finnegan drifted off into unconsciousness, although through his troubled dreams, he was sure he heard Woody calling for help, his cries weakening all the time.

"I've dealt with Vernon," Thaddeus said, returning to the chapel.

Randolph raised his eyebrows and broke off from the pleasant conversation he and Fergal were having with the weak but alert Maria.

"I'm surprised," he said, "that a man with a sword beat a man with a gun, again."

"Do not be, not when that man is a hero such as myself. I gave him a stark choice: be run out of town, or be run through with cold steel. He took one look at my bloodied sword and ran."

Fergal noted Thaddeus' blood-streaked face, reckoning that when faced by such a fearsome sight, he would probably have run too.

"We're obliged," Fergal said, offering a smile and then frowning. "So that just leaves Woody to placate."

"I will not rest until I have dealt with your final foe." Thaddeus walked purposefully from the chapel, his sword thrust out before him.

With the threat of the gun-toter dealt with, Randolph and Fergal left Maria with Ophelia and followed Thaddeus out of the chapel. To their surprise, when they emerged, Bishop Finnegan was making his uncertain way toward them. He was holding his head and having trouble walking.

They hurried over to help him, but before they reached him, Finnegan raised a hand.

"I'm fine," he said.

"What happened?" Fergal asked.

"Myself and Woody had some trouble." Finnegan glanced back at the stables and shrugged. "We were looking into his casket containing the Treasure of Saint Woody. Then I fell, or perhaps he attacked me . . . I'm not sure now. It's all slipping away from me like a dream . . ."

"Where is Woody?"

"He was in the stables, although when I came to, he'd gone."

"If he attacked you," Thaddeus said, brandishing his sword, "I will make him regret it."

"I'm sure he didn't try to hurt me intentionally." Finnegan gestured feebly and then took the sensible move of sitting on the chapel steps. "There was this great red light and . . ."

"Rest awhile," Fergal urged. "Maybe you'll remember everything that happened later."

Finnegan agreed, although he continued to shake his head and rub his brow as he tried to make sense of the incident.

With Thaddeus taking the lead, the others headed to the stables. Woody's wagon was still there with his casket sitting on the back, but nobody was around.

"Well, it's clear Woody's not here," Randolph said.

"A great red light," Thaddeus mused, "a bishop falling unconscious, a mysterious disappearance . . . some might think that another miracle."

"But it wasn't," Fergal said, pointing at the roofless stable. "Woody probably climbed over the wall and ran off."

"He can run, but he cannot escape cold steel." Thaddeus stalked off, his sword thrust aloft.

Randolph and Fergal watched him go, shaking their heads. Then they turned to Woody's wagon.

"If Woody's gone for good," Fergal said, "are we taking his casket with us when we leave?"

"No," Randolph said. "I've had enough of him and his treasure."

Fergal nodded as they turned to the door.

"So what are we doing now?"

Randolph considered as they slipped outside. Finnegan was sitting on the chapel steps, still shaking his head. Ophelia had brought Maria outside to enjoy the twilight and although she was still too weak to stand, she was looking around with wonder at her first sight of Sundown in two years.

Randolph sighed. "There's nothing more for us to do here. We helped Maria. We helped Ophelia. We saved the mission. So we should move on."

"Agreed," Fergal said. "But only after we've let Oliver out of the storeroom."

Chapter Sixteen

After leaving Bishop Finnegan at the train station in Shinbone, Oliver Rhinehart brought his new wagon to a halt outside Milton's Saloon.

He went inside. The presence of a stage at the back of the saloon cheered him, so he hailed the barkeep.

"I'm Oliver Rhinehart," he said, walking to the bar. "You may have heard of me."

"Nope," Milton said.

Oliver bit his lip to avoid smiling. "In that case I have an offer of a lifetime that'll double your income."

Milton sighed. "What'll it cost me?"

"A room and fifty percent of the additional income I generate."

"I might be in the mood for negotiation after you've told me what you're offering."

Oliver leaned forward. "I'm offering Oliver Rhinehart's amazing Treasure of Saint Woody."

Milton snorted. "For a room, that treasure had better be pretty amazing."

"The Treasure of Saint Woody is a closed box." Oliver wrapped a conspiratorial arm around Milton's shoulders. "People pay for a chance to open it, and the first person who does gets an amazing surprise he, or she, will never forget . . ."

"Just one man," Vernon Black said to himself. "And he doesn't look like trouble."

Beside the campfire a sole man sat. He was poking the fire while turning a spitted rabbit, but he paused when Vernon's heavy footfalls sounded. From under a lowered brim, the man glared around, while his other hand inched toward the rifle at his side.

Vernon moved into the campfire light with his hands raised high, but the man still grabbed his rifle and swirled it round to aim at him.

"Step all the way into the light where I can see you, stranger," he said, "or die where you stand."

Vernon raised his hands and took a pace toward the fire.

"Whoa there, friend. I'm not trouble. I just want to share your heat and companionship for the night, if you don't mind."

The man gestured with his rifle, signifying that Vernon could come closer, but then instantly returned his aim to Vernon's chest.

"I'll believe you, but your first wrong move will be your last."

"Those aren't friendly words on such a pleasant night." Vernon craned his head back and gestured at the stars burning down from the crisp, clear night sky. "Stars are bright on nights like this. And on such nights, trouble never happens."

The man lowered his rifle. "That's poetic."

"I find inspiration in the stars." Vernon pointed to the east. "For instance, that's Orion, the gunslinger. That's my favorite. Then above Orion, there's Taurus, the rampaging longhorn. I like that one too, because that's my birth sign."

"You seem knowledgeable about such things," the man said, his voice losing its suspicious tone.

"I am." With his hands held wide, Vernon sat on the opposite side of the fire and smiled. "All the stars have a story to tell."

The man placed his rifle on the ground. "Then tell me more, friend."

Gunshots echoed down Sundown's main drag.

Two riders galloped through town. They fired into the air and hollered as they hurtled past the mission. Then they roared back through town on a second pass.

Outside El Hombre, a circle of cowhands surrounded a fight where two men were slugging it out, settling who had won their last hand of poker. The new saloon owner, Tucker Moorhead, tried to break up the fight, but when he failed, he shrugged and joined in.

Across the road, the Mission Saloon was advertising tonight's performance: THADDEUS T. THACKENBACKER THE THIRD, RACONTEUR OF HEROIC TALES, AND THE WEST'S GREATEST LIVING SWORDSMAN. But the saloon itself was empty.

Father Stone stood outside his empty chapel, contemplating his new challenge.

"So," he asked, "is it always like this?"

"No," Ophelia said. "Usually it's noisier."

"But not in the chapel," Sister Maria said.

"I can walk!" Randolph cried out, thrusting his arms aloft in triumph. "It's a miracle."

Fergal held Randolph's arm, helping him take his first tentative steps, but when he was sure he could walk on his own, he stood back to face the gathered audience.

"As you can see, no injury is so bad, no ailment is so painful, no condition is so embarrassing that this amber liquid cannot cure," Fergal announced. He held a bottle of his tonic aloft and shook it, letting the amber liquid cast sparkling light over the mass of skeptical faces. "And this miraculous cure can be yours for only a dollar."

"That didn't look like a miracle to me," a man on the front row said.

"Why not?" Fergal asked, as Randolph demonstrated his newfound mobility by dancing a jig.

"I know all about miracles, and your miracle was nothing like the one at the Mission Santa Maria."

Randolph stopped in midstep with a foot raised. Fergal set his hands on his hips.

"I've come from the Mission Santa Maria and I can assure you that Maria doesn't perform miracles."

"I'm not talking about Maria. I mean Saint Woody."

"Saint Woody?" Fergal spluttered.

"Sure. I heard that people were calling him a saint even when he was still among us. And that was before he made that eclipse miss the town. Then, before a renowned bishop, he disappeared in a blinding flash of red light, leaving behind a mysterious closed casket and a promise that he would return only when someone found a way to open the casket."

"He did disappear." Fergal waited until the man smiled in triumph. "He jumped over a wall."

The man snorted. "You shouldn't be rude about a saint and his miracle."

"There was no saint and there was no miracle." As the heckler continued to complain, Fergal looked at Randolph and uttered a long sigh. "I reckon we need to head farther away from Sundown."

"Agreed," Randolph said, moving to pack away their show. "I reckon it'll be a miracle if we never hear of miracles again."